THE SECRET OF
SEA-DREAM HOUSE

By ALBERT PAYSON TERHUNE

A Novel

I0632261

British Library Cataloguing-in-Publication Data
A catalogue record for this book is available from
the British Library

Albert Payson Terhune

Albert Payson Terhune was born on 21st December 1872, in New Jersey, United States. Terhune's father was the Reverend Edward Payson Terhune and his mother, Mary Virginia Hawes, was a writer of household management books and pre-Civil War novels under the name Marion Harland. He was one of six children, having four sisters and one brother, but only two of his sisters survived until adulthood. Further tragedy beset the family when his own wife, Lorraine Bryson Terhune, died four days after giving birth to their only child. He later remarried Anice Terhune, but had no more children.

Terhune received a Bachelor of Arts degree from Columbia University in 1893. The following year, he took a job as a reporter at the New York newspaper *The Evening World*, a position he held for the next twenty years. During this period, he began to publish works of fiction, such as *Dr. Dale: A Story Without A Moral* (1900), *The New Mayor* (1907), *Caleb Conover, Railroader* (1907), and *The Fighter* (1909). However, it was his short stories about his collie Lad, published in *Red Book*, *Saturday Evening Post*, *Ladies' Home*

Journal, *Hartford Courant*, and the *Atlantic Monthly*, that brought him mainstream success. A dozen of these tales were collected in to novel form and released as *Lad: A Dog* in 1919. This was a best-seller and in 1962 was adapted into a feature film. He went on to produce over thirty novels focussing on the lives of dogs and enjoyed much success in the genre.

Terhune's interest in canines was by no means restricted to fiction. He became a celebrated dog-breeder, specialising in rough collies, lines of which still exist in the breed today. Sunnybank kennels were the most famous collie kennels in the United States and the estate is now open to the public and known as Terhune Memorial Park. Terhune died on 18th February 1942 and was buried at the Pompton Reformed Church in Pompton Lakes, New Jersey.

MY BOOK
IS DEDICATED TO

THE THREE DEAR PEOPLE
OF "LOS INCAS"

AND TO THE MAGIC MEMORY OF
A NIGHT ON THE LAXAHATCHEE
—AND OF A SONG IN THE DARK

The Secret of
Sea-Dream House

The Background

Señor Don Lopez de Savedra does not come into the bulk of this story. He died nearly two hundred years before Saul Tevvis hunted ghosts and treasure and the Impossible, through the echoing moldiness of Sea-Dream House.

Yet if it had not been for Señor Don Lopez de Savedra we should have had no story; Sea-Dream House never would have risen fairy-like from the waterside jungle; and Invisible Terror would not have crawled there.

So be patient while de Savedra struts his brief five minutes before our curtain. He is well worth meeting and his tale is worth the telling. Be patient, and in turn I will be brief.

Señor Don Lopez de Savedra left Spain a single jump ahead of the Inquisition's officers. He took passage, by stealth, for the brave West Indies, in the days when the Spanish Main was just beginning to earn its blood-gold glamour. After a decade of dubiety, Savedra emerged into fame as super-buccaneer, letters of marque bearer, a sublimated pirate of much prowess and shrewdness.

The story of those ten silent years would be better worth your reading than what followed; even as a climb is better worth the recounting than are one's dizzy experiences on the summit. But, unluckily, no record of them can be found. So let us forget them and meet the pirate-extraordinary once more when he is at the blood-splashed peak of his career. This in the first quarter of the seventeenth century.

Now the average pirate of that day comes down to us haloed in an aureate glow. As a matter of fact, the average pirate was merely a navigant yeggman, who spent his life between the vocation of annexing precarious loot and the avocation of drinking up its proceeds. He died broke or on a rope.

But Savedra was to the average pirate what Napoleon was to the everyday Corsican bandit. Savedra won vast plunder and he won it by a queer mixture of audacity and genius. Moreover, he laid by carefully all he won. In another decade or so he was fabulously rich. Then it was he decided to retire and to live the life of an Old World nobleman.

His heaviest pillaging had been among British ships and British coast towns along the Main. England, now, was Spain's friend and ally. Moreover, there were rumors of Spanish galleons ransacked; and there was still that ancient charge against him which had made him flee Spain. Thus, altogether, it would be anything but safe for him to retire to his native land and there to set up grandee life with a purchased title and a purchased castle. His dream must be fulfilled elsewhere.

His ambition shifted and imagination took a hand. He resolved to create for himself in the New World a wilderness palace, there to reign as crownless king of whatsoever region he might pick out for the site of his home. The Spanish Main was growing too populous for his purpose. Also, the law was gaining a tight and tighter grip there. The law did not smile upon Señor Don Lopez de Savedra. He must look farther afield.

On a day, he had run up a south Florida inlet, to make safe a prize cargo and to elude the king's ships which just then were taking a more than neighborly interest in him. At the end of the inlet he had come upon a river, narrow, twisting, jungle-bordered, inexpressibly wild and beautiful.

It ran through the heart of the Seminole country to the north of the dreary Everglades; in an earthly paradise. Far up the river stood a knoll, well wooded and with an ice-bright and ice-cold spring at its base.

In the back of his brain Savedra had cherished the memory of the fairy-like spot. Now it recurred to him in a twinge of inspiration as an ideal site for his wilderness palace.

The difficulties were few for a dreamer with Savedra's ships and ingenuity and man-power and enormous wealth. In this subtropic wild he would rear himself a wonder-house. Here, among the savages and the blacks and the few far-scattered white folk, he would stand forth as a wilderness demigod.

With ludicrous ease, through the bribing of the right officials, he obtained a grant to the whole river and for a mile or so back of it in either direction, a grant as solidly legal as ever were letters-patent. The back-country of Florida was all but unexplored and was deemed of no present or future worth. Even a lesser man than the puissant Savedra would have had little trouble in securing the land-grant.

Next he proceeded to the building of his palace.

After the manner of other New World empire-designers, he made an alliance with the local sachem of the Seminoles, one Laxahatchee, whose people reverenced their chief as a deity. Thereby, much of the problem of labor and of transportation was solved. A captured ship-load of New Guinea blacks supplied the remainder of the unskilled labor. Artisans and clever craftsmen were lured thither by pledge of huge pay, from Kingston and from Port Royal and from many another seaport.

A famed English architect, sent to plan a new and ornate Government House at Jamaica, was bought away from his mission and was set to work on the designing of Savedra's forest palace. Curio shops in every port were ransacked and emissaries were dispatched to Europe for fittings and furnishings. For Savedra had a high, if garish, ideal for his palace's equipment.

Raid after raid did he make upon defenseless regions of the West Indies, where men of taste and of wealth had built mansions for themselves. The best and the rarest things from these houses were borne away to beautify the Florida palace.

But his most daring and brutal and successful foray was upon the shining white house of John Tallbot, high upon the green hilltop to south of Kingston Harbor.

Tallbot had chanced to meet Savedra, years agone, and imprudently had invited the corsair to his house. Thither, again and again, Savedra had come as a guest, lured and dazzled by the exquisite beauty of its interior. Now,

once more, he called there, this time uninvited
and at dead of night and with forty stout
rogues at his back. The rest was Horror.

Tallbot was old, rich, eccentric, a dilettante.
Bad lungs had brought him from his Shrop-
shire manor to this sunlit Jamaica hilltop. He
had borne along with him his household gods
and the mementoes of his wide travels. Here
he had settled, above the jade-and-sapphire sea.
In wrought-silver letters on a carven bronze
tablet above his door he had caused to be
blazoned the name of his white home: "SEA-
DREAM HOUSE."

Tallbot had been attracted first to Savedra
—though presently he sickened of the swagger-
ing super-pirate's grim presence in his lovely
house—because of the buccaneer's name, and
because Don Lopez was a kinsman and a boy-
hood playmate of the man whom Tallbot admired most in the world—Miguel de Savedra
Cervantes, the wonder-writer whose *Don Quixote* had "laughed away the chivalry of Spain."

To his guest, Tallbot had talked with eager
enthusiasm about Cervantes, showing him let-

ters and fragments of manuscript which the master had sent to his English worshiper from time to time. Savedra had yawned until his jaws cracked, at Tallbot's eulogies of a poky old fellow who could find no more manly means for a livelihood than to scribble foolish tales and verses and such trash. But, ever, as he yawned, his vulture eyes were preying avidly among the beautiful things which filled Sea-Dream House's low-raftered rooms.

As a net result of Savedra's uninvited nocturnal visit to the white house on the hilltop, Tallbot lay across his own doorway with six inches of steel in his wizened throat. Forty men under Savedra's direction carried to the harbor forty loads of rich possessions whose seizure had gutted the hilltop house as thoroughly as though fire had scourged it.

Last of all in the laden procession swaggered Señor Don Lopez de Savedra. Carelessly he stepped over the body of his dead host and victim. The house's carven Florentine church doors already had been lifted from their hinges and were on their way down the hill.

As he crossed the threshold, Savedra raised one mighty hand and wrenched from its screws the bronze tablet bearing the silver-lettered words, "SEA-DREAM HOUSE." He liked the name. He liked the tablet. What Savedra liked he took.

In the hot, mystic heart of the south Florida jungle, the new wilderness mansion took form and bulk. Sweating Seminoles, grunting and scourged negro slaves, toiled at forced draft in its building. Craftsmen earned and double-earned their high wages, under Savedra's arrogant urgence for speed. Ships from Europe, laden with material and with furnishings, anchored off the inlet, whence Indian flatboats transferred the cargoes upriver to the knoll-foot.

An Italian landscape gardener was sent for, to lay out the grounds and to bring along from Italy tons of ancient carved marble for summer-houses and pools and statuary. The English architect threw himself heart and soul into the execution of Savedra's bizarre wishes. For here money was no object; and the architect was a poor man, despite his fame and skill.

The erstwhile jungle silences were smashed by incessant hammer-blows and by the roaring of orders. Over all brooded Savedra's dominating presence and mastery. Daily he evolved new ideas, new fancies. His early memories of certain of the more intricate castles of his homeland were revived, as regarded secret passages and invisible stairways and other melodramatic features, some of which his architect could compass and some of which he could not.

Meantime, as one sovereign with another, he and the stately Laxahatchee conferred and collogued and drank deep. The Seminole was vastly impressed by his new white neighbor's wealth and power. Savedra endured the savage because for the time he needed him.

Then there was a hint of trouble from various members of Savedra's crew. For years these men had sailed with their grim master, risking life and liberty at his nod. Now, like old dogs, they hung about him, unable to consider life away from his long dominance. And as an impatient man might stone an undesired dog which insisted on following him, so did Savedra scatter wrathfully this remnant of his followers, who had not taken themselves off at his behest, as had the rest of his men.

He reminded them that they had been paid and dismissed, and he swore he was not going to have them hanging onto his bounty, in his new grandeur, like shabby ravens at a feast. Curtly and with great force he bade them go to hell. And they went—if not to the destination suggested by Savedra, at least slinkingly out of his ken. More than one of them breathed rum-flavored threats of reprisal against the man who had made his wealth through them and who then had kicked them out.

At last the wilderness wonder-house was completed, inside and out—completed wellnigh to Savedra's liking. As a finishing touch, Don Lopez bade one of his men climb above the front doors—the carven church doors he had lifted from their wrought-iron hinges at Tallbot's house—and to screw there the bronze tablet with its silvern legend, "SEA-DREAM HOUSE."

He had rejected one magniloquent title after another for his new home. At last it had occurred to him that it could have no more poetical name than Tallbot had given to a similarly beautiful abode. So "Sea-Dream House" it was; and a cask of priceless ancient Xeres was broached, by way of baptism.

The craftsmen and the landscape man and the architect were dismissed; their pockets gravid with gold pieces. Down the river they were sent in a crowded longboat toward the inlet mouth, where waited the ship which was to carry them overseas. Seminoles rowed the laden boat. These same Seminoles took a wrong turning at one of the score of places where creeks and brooks debouch in a snakelike tangle into the main river.

There, the boat, clumsily handled, stuck on a sandbar. Thither, at nightfall, before the craft could be floated free, swarmed a half-hundred painted Indians who overcame and massacred the entire boatload of workers.

Next morning, Laxahatchee appeared a
Dream House, bearing with him great baḡ
of gold—the contents of the slain artificers'
pockets, the accumulated pay for their labors.
According to agreement, he prepared to count
it out and then to divide it equally with his
revered friend, Señor Don Lopez de Savedra.

But Savedra was a thrifty soul. True, he
was glad to have saved, with Laxahatchee's
kind help, the wages he had promised and had
paid to his craftsmen. It had been a veritable
inspiration of his, this massacre which so easily
could be laid to unknown savages, in case of
investigation.

But he saw no reason why he should share
the pile of hard-earned and hard-recovered gold
with a mere Indian sachem, simply because he
had promised to do so. Wherefore, he suggested that a tenth of the loot would repay
Laxahatchee amply for the work his braves
had done in killing and robbing the boatload
of foreigners.

Laxahatchee could not see it that way. To
his childlike aboriginal soul a promise was a

promise and somehow was sacred. He said so. Savedra laughed heartily. The former pirate had a pretty sense of humor as well as of thrift.

The primitive Indian did not share this subtle appreciation of a jest. Indeed, when he found Savedra was proposing to scrap an agreement which the sachem had deemed sacred, and that he was to receive one-tenth instead of one-half the booty, Laxahatchee flew into a homicidal rage.

Thus much a listening servant heard and babbled of. But later when the same servant entered the room where the two over-lords had been squabbling, Savedra was sitting there alone. He was sipping reflectively at a jorum of cold punch and whiffing his long pipe of Barbados. Reclining thus in his cool withdrawing-room, in the heat of the day, he was every inch a landed proprietor.

Laxahatchee had gone. But whither Laxahatchee had gone no man knew. For he did not return as usual to his village, nor did mortal man of that century set eyes on him again. Mighty had been this arch-sachem of the Seminoles. Many and urgent were the inquiries made for him.

Savedra was questioned. He replied suavely that he and the chief had sat and drunk and smoked in the dimly cool withdrawing-room and that there they had spoken pleasantly of many things. Then, amid their expressions of mutual esteem, Laxahatchee had taken his leave. More than that, Savedra could not say; although he assured all concerned that his own heart was heavy within him for the disappearing of his well-loved friend.

Some believed. Some doubted. None dared accuse openly the lightning-tempered Spaniard. As a matter of fact, there was no direct proof to connect him with the passing of Laxahatchee. But it was not the first nor the tenth strange occurrence to center around Sea-Dream House. It served to swell the growingly sinister repute of the wilderness mansion.

The Seminoles glowered at the shining edifice as they paddled past it on the river. Such few members of Savedra's crew as lingered in the region spat and cursed as they went by it;

or as Don Lopez swept downstream in his eight-oared and gilt-prowed longboat or rode the trails on his giant black stallion with grooms and equerries at his heels.

Never, nowadays, did the Spaniard fare forth alone. He was a brave man, but he was no fool. He was enjoying this new life of his too much to risk losing it through the silent flutter of a poisoned Indian arrow amid the jungle foliage or by a knife-slash or a pistol-ball. Well enough did he know the truth of the Spanish proverb that threatened men live long. But even a proverb may fail of fulfill-ment. So he took no needless chances with his ever-increasing horde of Indian and white and half-breed haters.

More than once, efforts were made to sur-prise him in his own semi-fortified house. But those who came to slay crept tremblingly forth again with unbelievable tales of ghosts and the like. Nor would they or those who heard their stories go thither again.

Yet, on a morning, two years after he set-tled down to his life of ease and of lordship in

his glittering forest palace, Señor Don Lopez de
Savedra was found lying at the foot of his
grand staircase, stone dead and with an aspect
of stark agony etched deep into his bearded
face. There was no wound upon him.

His major-domo, a hairy giant named
Pariera, who had also been Savedra's mate and
his one trusted friend, seized upon his dead master's home and chattels and vowed to hold them,
by dint of brute force, against whatever next-of-
kin law the distant Spanish government might
invoke.

Pariera was as good as his word. He lorded
it in the bright abode, even as had Savedra.
But in less than a month he, too, lay dead at
the foot of the rich staircase, at dawn of a
spring morning, unwounded, but with his sallow face a mask of horrified anguish.

That was enough. The servants fled in mortal terror. The folk of the region shunned the
house as though it were the haunt of every
demon and hell-sprite in all Florida—as, indeed, most of them swore it was. Once or
twice, bold spirits dared the curse of the place

by breaking in to loot some of its priceless treasures.   But such deeds of plunder were few, and misfortune was said to have followed hot upon them.

Thus, the bright house aged into a whitened plague-spot; shunned and desolate.   The jungle pressed in on the smooth turf and on the sunken gardens and plaisaunces.   Generation after generation, in the sparse-settled neighborhood, repeated the olden horror-tales of it, with gruesome embellishments; and they gave the accursed place a wide berth.

Mold and rot and weather took their toll of the beautiful things which Savedra had brought from every quarter of the world to adorn his palace.   But almost no human hand took part in this gradual demolition.

Even the name-plate tablet above the exquisitely carved church doors hung unmolested. Its silvern letters, dull black with time and dampness, still spelled forth dankly the legend: "SEA-DREAM HOUSE."

Chapter One

SAUL TEVVIS sat reading that gloomy old tale, *Frankenstein*. Ten years agone, he had read it. Then, it had impressed him only as an original theme expressed in quaint phrasing. Now, he reread it because of a sudden it had become his own story and thus of morbid personal interest to him.

Even as young Frankenstein had created a monster which thenceforth threatened his maker's destruction, so had young Saul Tevvis wrought something which menaced his whole career.

At twenty-eight he had had the rare chance to write a novel which a tolerably large section of the reading world acclaimed. It sprang to the rank of a best seller and then to super-best seller in a bare handful of time. Solid critics and lesser and more hysterical reviewers hailed it as epoch-marking. Some of them heralded its amazed young author as the long-expected Great American Novelist.

Tevvis had slaved, night after night, for two years, after tiring days at a newspaper office, to evolve and to polish and to make perfect this book of his. He had not written it with any direct idea of gain, knowing well that the average novel brings scant fortune to its creator. He had written it because it clamored to be written and because to him its gradual creation was a pleasure akin to pain.

Then he sent his brain-child forth into the haunts of men, modestly hoping it might find a publisher and perhaps a few hundred readers.

The rest was ovation.

Checks poured in. Publishers and editors assailed him for his next novel. Interviewers thronged to him. People of consequence with whom he had had but a nodding acquaintance took him up with an adoring vehemence. The literary world stretched eager arms to him. The public sought him out anywhere and everywhere. He was lionized, flattered, overwhelmed.

For a time the wild adulation pleased him. It even mounted to his head. He could not understand it all, and he was glad to take his meed of fame's sweets. Then, bit by bit, it began to press in upon him like the slowly strangling mists of a night-mare.

Privacy was gone; leisure was gone; work-time was gone. No longer did he have an hour to himself. No longer could he fill his day-light hours with the work he loved. Every minute was claimed by outsiders and was frit-tered away by them. His loved book became to him a thing of horror; for to it he owed this eternal breath-taking cataract of publicity.

It was the monster which he, the twentieth-century Frankenstein, had created with bloody sweat and with pride, and which threatened to destroy everything that made his life worth living.

More—it threatened to slay something beau-tiful which was not yet created. In the back of Tevvis's brain a second novel was taking vaguely exquisite shape, was assuming more and more distinct form, more and more wondrous possibilities.

It was not to be the scramblingly-written and uninspired "second book" of a man who seeks to follow up a chance success. Rather was it to be the perfect logical successor and peer of his first brain-offspring.

But what chance was there for it to be born —or if born at all, what chance was there for it to assume the perfection that was its birthright? How could he sit down, for hours a day, and give to it the undisturbed and grippingly concentrated work which alone could make it what he dreamed it should be? All mankind was hounding him. His telephone jangled unceasingly. His mail was staggeringly huge and importunate. Visitors avalanched down upon him and would not be denied.

As easily write his wonder-book in the midst of a shell-scourged battlefield as in such surroundings as now were his. Either he must degenerate into a drawing-room-and-studio-tea lionet or he must get clear of everything and everybody and live alone for months with his new book; live with it and in it and for it, until it should be completed.

Always, when life pressed too closely on him, of old, Tevvis had dropped everything and had fared forth somewhere into the wilderness, there to fish or hunt or loaf or hike, until he should get his bearings once more.

He was not rich—or had not been until his royalty checks began to gush in—but he had had a very few thousand dollars a year beyond his earnings; enough to live as he chose to live, in a cozy little bachelor suite, waited on by Gedge, a stockily grumpy and grumpily stocky middle-aged English body servant whom Saul had inherited from his father, and with the worshiping chumship of Bunty, his honey-colored little bobtailed collie.

He had lived right pleasantly and busily, thus served and companioned, until the world had yanked him from his busy seclusion and had set him upon an Eiffel Tower of rackety notoriety.

Unspeakably he yearned to pull up stakes as

always before, and to hie him to some far-off spot where life was in the rough, there to get back his mental and moral balance and to rest his ears from the multiple bellow of applause. But the thing could not be done. He had become a public figure.

Let him dive into the Adirondack hinterland, into the Arizona sands, into the Rockies, into the Canadian backwoods. What would happen? The press would take up the hue-and-cry. Tuft-hunters would follow him, teasing his frayed nerves with their attentions. Local inhabitants would welcome him to their neighborhood and would flock to destroy his loneliness. He was a prisoner, the helpless captive to his own new-born fame.

Tevvis laid down *Frankenstein* and glowered miserably toward the kitchen of his suite, whence, of a sudden, right dolorous sounds began to issue. The sounds took form; and the form was rhythmic. The rhythm was of a song, chanted off key and with something the timbre of "Alberich's Curse." Tevvis grunted in dire annoyance and listened. Gedge

was enlivening the hours of toil by singing;
a hideous habit whereof Saul had striven
vainly to break him. Out drifted the words:

"W'en I heard he was merrid I uttered no moan,
For the eyes of all present was fixed on my own.
But I fled to my bowdoor to hide my despair
And I tore the rich suclet of gems from my hair.
But they . . . "

A double buzz of the suite's doorbell cut
short the ditty and sent the singer's ample feet
flap-flapping shufflingly down the hallway.

Not optimistic enough to hope the building's
other dwellers might be complaining of the
sour cacophony, Tevvis waited to learn what
new interruption the buzzer might have heralded. Then Gedge came into the room, both
hands gripping awkwardly a heterogeneous
mass of envelopes. The afternoon mail had
arrived, the lightest mail of the day, yet almost
too bulky for the Englishman's stubby fingers
to encircle.

Gedge made as though to lay it on the stand
beside Tevvis. The bunch of letters slipped,
eel-like, from his stiff grasp and cascaded over

Saul's lap, slithering thence to the wolf rug at his feet.

"Sorry, sir," mumbled Gedge, surlily.

"It's all right," answered Saul, eyeing glumly the scattered burden as his servant stooped gruntingly to scrape the envelopes together and put them back on the stand. "It's all right. No harm done. But you'd have made a real hit with me if you'd been reaching into the elevator shaft when you lost hold of them. It would have saved me an hour of boredom and ——"

His words trailed away. One of the letters had come to rest on his lap in its fall floorward. It lay with the superscription and the Italian postmark staring up at him. Back in the memory-swamps at the very base of Saul Tevvis's heart there was a twinge of faintly sick excitement at the sight.

Once that handwriting had thrilled him to the quick and had set his heart to beating foolishly. Now there was no thrill; no hot ecstasy of expectation; nothing but a stirring of dead and damped fires where only a forgotten ember or two scorched reminiscently into his soul.

He tore wide the thin envelope and pulled out the sheet of paper it held. His mouth twisting ever so little in a half-smile of self-disgust, he read:

SAUL:

Isn't it glorious? Oh, I'm so proud of you! But I always knew you were the most wonderful man on earth and I always knew everybody else would find it out some day. I am so happy—so happy not only for you, but for—*us!* I can still say that, can't I, dear? You still care, don't you—just as I still care and as always I must care?

We've been at the out-of-the-worldest place, clear back of Taormina, all season. It is supposed to be a palace, but it is more like a ruined catacomb. Dad took it for the fall and winter, but three months of it was all any of us could stand, so we're starting home.

It wasn't till I got to Naples, yesterday, that I heard of anything that has happened in the outside world. Then I ran across the Pardfields and they told me about your magnificent success. Meta Pardfield had a copy of your book and she lent it to me and I read it all night. Saul, it's—*supreme!* She says you're the most-talked-of man in América just now, and that you'll probably clean up almost a million dollars from your royalties and the movies and the dramatic rights and all.

That part of it didn't mean anything at all to me. You know that. I was only proud that you're getting such gorgeous recognition. But I *am* so proud and so happy that your dreams have come true—your dreams of literary success and of money and of fame and everything.

There's another dream of ours that can come true, Saul, if you still want it to. We're sailing on the *Conte Rosso*, Tuesday. I'll be in New York by the time this letter gets to you, or a day or two later, anyway. We're going to stop for a week at the St. Crœsus while we look for a house. You'll call up there and find just the minute we're expected? But I know you will. And I can see you dropping this scrawl of a letter and reaching for the phone to find from the steamship people just when the *Conte Rosso* will dock.

I'll be watching for you, dear, at the rail. And I'll pick out your face from all the ocean of faces on the pier. It will be my heart, and not just my eyes, that will know where to look for you, Saul. And when we are together, no foolish misunderstanding is ever going to separate us again. That's a promise, wonder-boy of mine.

Perhaps I ought not to be writing this way. But your marvelous book has made me dizzy and it has enthralled me. And I'm just a little bit fey at the knowledge that I'm going to see you again. Oh,

Saul ——! Never mind, I'll wait and say it, instead of writing it. I'll say it in a whisper. But you'll hear. For we'll be *very VERY* close together, you and I, when it's said.

Yours—oh, *terribly* much yours, if you still want me (Do you?)——

BAB.

Twice Saul Tevvis's eyes traversed grimly the closely written lines. Then, very slowly, he tore the letter into tiny irregular white bits. The fragments strayed from between his loose-held fingers and trailed to the wolf rug, whence Gedge had just salvaged the last of the scattered envelopes. The stocky man-servant peered down at the new litter in silent reproach.

"Never mind, Gedge," soothed Tevvis. "I'm a careless cuss. Don't bother. I'll pick it up myself. Do you know what that white stuff is, down there on the rug—the stuff I dropped just now?"

"I do, sir," sniffed Gedge, his orderly spirit deeply outraged. "I do, indeed. I haven't picked up after you for twenty-odd years, not to know. It's a mess of torn paper bits for rheumatic old fingers to clean up. Because, for all you say you'll do it yourself, I know fine and well you won't remember to. Yes, I do know what it is, sir. It's more work; like it always is. When it isn't paper scraps, it's cigar butts and filthy ashes, or else it's pipe tobacco. It's always something. And your father such a neat gentleman, too! He ———"

"Yes, yes," hastily interrupted Saul. "I seem to have heard something like that a few hundred times before. Sometimes I wonder whether you're my fairly efficient servant, Gedge, or whether you're my cranky old nurse. Anyhow, run on now. I have some writing to do. Wait, though. You made a bad guess when I asked you what that stuff was on the floor. You think it is a handful of torn paper. But that's because you do all your seeing with your eyes and none of it with your imagination. That's the torn-up particles of a dream, Gedge. A dream that started out to be pure gold and wound up by being dross and shag-lead, mixed. That's what it is."

"Up to the time folks began making such

a fuss over you, sir," rebuked Gedge, "I never saw you take hardly a sip of liquor. But you've sure been taking too much to-day, to be talking nonsense like that, if I may make so bold as to say so. 'Dreams'!"

"Dreams!" echoed Tevvis, his thoughts straying. "Dreams. Sea-dreams. Sea-Dream House."

"Begging pardon, sir?" queried Gedge, puzzled.

Saul Tevvis came out of his brief reverie with a start.

"I just happened to remember a queer name," he explained, abashed before his old servant's reproving stare. "It's a name I ran across a couple of years ago. That time I dropped my work and ran away from New York and went bass-fishing in Florida. The time I took Bunty along and she got bitten by that rattlesnake and nearly died. I told you about it. She ——"

"You did, sir," assented Gedge, still on the defensive. "But what's it got to do with a litter of paper scraps that I'll have to get down on my knees and clean away and that you call 'sea-dreams' ——"

"It was a name above the door of a queer old haunted house up on the Laxahatchee River. I blundered onto it by chance, while I was fishing the upper reaches of the river. It's a paradise for bass and it's miles out of the world. When I was speaking to you about dreams, just now, the name popped into my head. It —— By the way, speaking of running away, I've got to do it again. First, because I can't work if I don't. Second, because if I don't ——"

His eyes strayed worriedly to the torn letter at his feet and the sentence died unfinished. Gedge waited in sulky patience for an instant. As Tevvis did not speak again, but sat frowning down at the torn paper, the servant prepared to take himself aggrievedly out of the room. At the doorway he cleared his throat and said, coldly:

"If all this crazy telephoning and visits and letters and reporter-men keeps up, the best thing we both can do is to run away, as you call it. I'm fair sick and pestered with it all."

"That is because you have waxed famous, Gedge," replied Tevvis, solemnly, "and because you aren't geared to bask in the sunshine of fame. You yearn to blush unseen—if at all. Perhaps we'll both run away, if we can find a place to run to, where nobody can follow us. Know of any such place, Gedge? If you do ——"

"From all you say, sir," suggested Gedge, taking Saul's words, as ever, in entire seriousness, "you'd be fair well hid in some hole like this here Sea-Dream House you were talking about. Didn't you just say it's 'miles out of the world'? And ——"

"Quite," agreed Tevvis. "But it's too near Palm Beach and the crowds. There was a chap named Emerson who said if a man makes a better mousetrap than anybody else can make, and if he hides in the woods, the world will wear a path to his door. So ——"

"Maybe they would, at that, sir," considered Gedge, thoughtfully. "I never yet saw a mousetrap that was worth a clipped farthing. And if anyone was to make a real good mouse-trap, I ain't saying but what I'd maybe go hunt him up, myself, mice being my aversion. But if it's only just a silly thing like writing a book —begging your pardon—I can't see why folks should go into the woods looking for the man who wrote it. There's lots of books. Besides, if you didn't want 'em to follow you up, it'd be simple enough to stop 'em."

"Tell me how, oh, most wise Gedge," demanded Tevvis, "and I'll give you half my kingdom. It ——"

"There was my mother's uncle, now," explained Gedge, "him that was the black sheep of the family. Higgs his name was. He was took before the beaks on a charge of stealing a watch. Back in 1871, it was. Higgs left the court without a stain on his character, but with a warning not to be seen there again. He was living just off Mile End Road at the time, I call to mind. Well, next week a copper comes down their alley, asking impudent questions about him. It seems there had been another pickpocket job pulled off and there was unworthy suspicions of my great-uncle. What does my great-uncle do? He skips off to Manchester, and there he gets a job in one of the iron furnaces, and he changes his name from Higgs to Blawley. And that throws the coppers off. They send word to the police at Manchester and a lot of other places to be on the lookout for one Higgs. But they don't know about Blawley. So my great-uncle's as safe as safe. That is, he is till he gets into new trouble over a wallet that he finds. If you want to get away from folks, sir, go some'rs and take a new name. That's my advice."

Ashamed of his own unwonted garrulity, Gedge retreated to his pantry, leaving Tevvis staring interestedly after him. Saul was doing quick and eager thinking. The tale of the unregenerate Higgs-Blawley had given him a genuine inspiration.

He turned back to his desk and scribbled a long and circumstantial letter to Musgrave Herne, his former classmate and present man of business. Swearing Herne to secrecy, he bade him get in touch with his firm of Florida correspondents, through them to find if Sea-Dream House and its grounds could be leased for the rest of the winter and the spring.

If so [continued the letter], get it for me, under the name of—of Garry Keith—and don't let even your Florida people know my real name. I'll send Gedge down there to clean things up a bit and provision the old ruin and lay in what little extra furniture, etc., we may need. Then I'll follow, and spend the winter there with Gedge to look after me and with Bunty for housemate.

It is a gaudy inspiration, and it flashed on me, full grown, just now while Gedge was blithering away at me. It's the only way I can get clear from everyone and do some real work on this new book that's begging me to write it. It will mean months of perfect seclusion, perfect aloneness, perfect concentration. I'll lug along my easel and my paints, as a blind. So, give it out that I'm an eccentric artist down there to do some sketches of the backwoods.

The Laxahatchee and the land close to it are the only part of Florida, so far as I've seen, where the realtor hasn't tried to make the wilderness blossom like the fifth proposition of Euclid. It's still wild and desolate—the only place on earth where I can bury myself and write, unpestered. Try to get me the lease of the Sea-Dream House, won't you, if it can possibly be done? I heard, when I was down there, that it belonged nominally to a Madrid estate and that some agents in Palm Beach have the handling of it.

The more I think of this thing the more lure it has for me. But if it's guessed that I'm there, goodby to any chance of working! It's less than thirty miles from Palm Beach and every loafing friend of mine and every Palm Beach lion-chaser will be swarming all over me.

I'm going to give out an interview and say I'm on my way to some unheard-of foreign place—Abyssinia sounds remote enough—for the rest of the season; to study native conditions. Any kind of notoriety stunt will be swallowed. Then I'll sneak down to the Laxahatchee and do the best work I've ever done. I rely on your word not to tell a soul where I am or who "Garry Keith" is. Rush it, won't you? I'll pay extra cash for extra speed. This daffy conglomeration here in New York is doing things to my nerves. I want to hide.

So delighted was Tevvis with his marvelous new plan and at the prospect it held out for work and for privacy, that he forgot the very existence of the riffle of paper scraps on the floor beside his desk. But as he sealed and addressed his epistle to Musgrave Herne, his glance fell afresh upon them; and he recalled what they stood for. The glint of boyish anticipation died from his eyes as he brooded upon the fragments of the letter whose reading had filled him with that strange ghost of a pang.

A ball of blond fur, reposing on the corner of the study couch, uncurled itself lazily, resolving into an undersized and over-fluffy yellow collie. She stretched herself, one dainty white leg after another, then jumped down from the couch and trotted gayly across to where Saul Tevvis stood. Bunty, his bobtailed and fiery little chum, had wakened from her afternoon nap and was anxious to set forth on her usual ramble through the Park.

She thrust her pointed nose insinuatingly into her master's hand. Then, as he still stared worriedly down at the strewn bits of paper, she galloped into the hallway, presently returning with his hat held mincingly between her jaws. Tevvis laughed, patting her head and looking amusedly into the eager brown eyes upraised to his.

"Not just yet, Bunty," he said, speaking as

if to a fellow-human. "Presently we'll get our hike. I have a letter to write first, Bunty. Another letter. A rotten letter. But when one has to operate, it's best to do it in a single slash. Then it's done. If one hesitates, the whole wretched job has to be done all over again. Especially when a woman is mixed up in it, Bunty. It's one of the times when a man has to be either a rabbit or a rattlesnake. You've chased a hundred rabbits, Bunty, girl, and you were bitten by one rattlesnake. So you ought to know what I'm talking about. She'll get me unless I cut loose—unless I cut loose without leaving one strand of the cable uncut. You remember how it was before, Bunty. I was the unhappiest man in seven states. I'm not going to be again, if I can get away quickly enough and far enough. Even the man-devouring Barbara Crale isn't going to smash my heart a second time. Get that, Bunty?"

At each purposed repetition of her name, Bunty wagged vehemently her half-length mop of a tail and did queer little grace-note steps as she danced around the speaker. Like many another lonely man, Saul Tevvis had drifted into the habit of talking to this collie chum of his as though she could understand all he said.

Now he sat down at the desk again, and, squaring his wide young shoulders for an ordeal, he began to write.

DEAR BARBARA [his note began]:

I can't answer your letter in its own key, so I am going to be perhaps brutally frank. Here goes:

Two years ago you were unwise enough to en-gage yourself to me, though you were the most popu-lar girl and the most attractive girl I had known; and though I was a third-rater whose income and newspaper salary wouldn't have paid for the kind of clothes you like to wear.

Six months later you found out your mistake and you were sensible enough to throw me over. I won't bore you by telling how it hurt, or how the old scar still throbs at times. You threw me over because Colvin Leland was blind in love with you and be-cause he had an income that made mine look like the change left from a plugged dime. (Yes, that is a brutal way to put it, I know; but you admitted it, yourself, when I was so insane and noisy in beseech-ing you not to give me up.) He was a *parti*. I was only a party.

Six months ago Colvin Leland went down with his yacht off Point Judith. It was just after his death that you met Prince Angelini. Angelini fell in love with you. Most men do, I find. He was that rare exotic, a foreign prince with a real income. To make sure of becoming a genuine *principessa* you took your family to Sicily and made them rent a villa near his estates.

Last month, I read in *City Cuttings* the sordid little statement that a wife had turned up, whom Angelini had married in Brazil. As he is not of rank that permits of morganatic marriages, your campaign was at an end. That is why you are coming back to America.

Then you happen to find out that an odd twist of luck has made me momentarily famous and has given me more money than I used to believe was coined. Hence your letter to me.

I think I have summed up the whole situation, truthfully, if baldly. The only thing left to say is that I don't care to enter the lists again. If that is a brutal way of putting it, I ask your forgiveness. I am about to leave town, and I shall not have the good fortune to see you before I go. I'm sorry I couldn't have said all these things more gently; but if I had I should have left a loophole for more misery and heartache to seep through.

Chapter Two

THREE weeks later the newspapers carried
stories of varying length about an eccentric plan announced by the great Saul Tevvis.
In the very acme of his fame and prestige, the
young genius was about to turn his back on
America and on the fruits of his success. He
was going to set forth to Abyssinia, there to
spend some months in the back country, far
from the coast and farther from reach of
civilization.

It seemed he had always been keenly interested in this little-exploited land and that he
believed he could gather material there for a
wholly original type of novel. Deliberately he
was going to cut himself off from his friends
and from all contact with his former life and
was going to plunge into the Abyssinian hinterland, where mail and cable could not reach
him. He was going to live like a native and

wholly among the natives. Several of the papers hinted broadly that it was a mighty clever publicity stunt and that if he could succeed in running into danger in Abyssinia, it would have splendid press value for his next book.

Thus it was that Saul Tevvis vanished from New York in the heyday of his popularity. Thus it was that "Garry Keith" boarded a night express for Florida on the same day that the young author was supposed to be sailing from Boston on the first lap of his perilous Abyssinian journey.

Musgrave Herne had done his work quickly and well. Thanks to his enterprise and to the efforts of his Florida agents, Sea-Dream House had been leased for a term of six months by a New York artist, Garry Keith by name, who sought local color for a series of jungle-and-river paintings.

There had been no complications about securing the lease; nor had the price been exorbitant. Thanks to its tumble-down condition and remoteness and to the sinister rumors which clung to every inch of it, Sea-Dream House had gone tenantless since the long-ago day of Pariera's death. Nobody wanted it.

The property, after much search by eighteenth-century advocates, had been settled upon an obscure Madrid family, the nearest living relatives of Savedra. Unwanted, and useless as a revenue-producer, it had remained in the family for nearly two hundred years. Successive Spanish heirs had paid the negligible taxes, more through clan pride and for the sake of bragging of a vast ancestral estate in the Americas than from any tangible hope of gain. The agents were overjoyed at a chance to make even a small sum from its occupancy.

Gedge had been sent down to the Laxahatchee with trunkfuls of necessaries and followed by innumerable crates and boxes of provisions, to make habitable the few rooms he and Tevvis might need and to prepare for his employer's coming. Bunty had been sent thither with him.

Strangely enough, the grouchily conservative old Englishman was actually enthusiastic about the scheme. Perhaps a drop of lawless blood —a throwback to the lamentable Higgs-Blawley—stirred within him at the idea of his young employer going under an alias and hiding himself from the rest of mankind. In any event, he entered into the preparations with a zest.

Saul himself was thrilled by prospect of the bizarre adventure. He boarded the Florida train as a schoolboy might embark on a treasure-quest. He slept like a child, in the comfortless drawing room he had engaged. Next morning, as he dressed, he gazed out at the flat Carolina landscape, as at a new world.

Level gray fields; pine barrens; black cabins with black folk in their dooryards and black mules tethered to black sheds; lazy hamlets; sleeping farms that waited the touch of spring to bourgeon into rich wakefulness—all had an air of novelty and romance to the city-jaded and over-lionized Tevvis.

In leisurely fashion he dressed and shaved, and then made his way forward to the dining car. Just ahead of him a girl was going from the observation platform to one of the forward cars.

She walked with a singular freedom of gait and light poise, despite the sway of the train. Lithe she was, and slender and small, and dainty, yet with an outdoor hint in figure and in bearing. Her bronze hair was piled high in shimmering masses on her regal little head. She glanced sidelong at the view from one of the windows, and Saul was aware of a deliciously irregular profile and a piquancy of expression.

Then she reached her own car, and stood with her back to him, arranging a coat that had fallen from her chair. Perforce, Tevvis moved on, seeing her no more. She was not in that same car when he came back from breakfast.

Oddly, the memory of her recurred to Saul more than once during the long day. He was amused at himself, and mildly vexed, that the figure and profile and free motion of a wholly unknown girl should stick in his mind.

Barbara Crale was the only woman who had

made any deeply lasting impression on him, in all the few years of his manhood. He was not susceptible. That was why his unhappy love affair with Barbara had cut so deep and why he was so fiercely resolved not to run the minutest risk of incurring future pain by remaining within danger of meeting her again. He knew now that his despairing grief at her desertion of him had been a sharper wound to vanity than to heart and that his wild love for her had been more infatuation than anything bigger.

Yet he had made grim decision that women henceforth should mean nothing to him. That was why he was scornfully amused at himself and growingly annoyed when the image of this dainty stranger refused to depart from his thoughts.

That evening, on his way to the dining car, he met her, face to face. It was for only an instant, in the narrow passageway alongside a clump of drawing rooms. He stood close to the wall to give her room to pass, and she inclined her head slightly in recognition of the courtesy.

That was all. She did not even look at him, nor notice more than that some fellow-passenger was giving her the right of way. Yet the lights fell softly on her high-bred little face, and Tevvis had a clear if momentary view of it.

He had seen a hundred women more classically beautiful and another hundred who were more bewitchingly pretty. But there was an elfin quality to her expression, a childlike simplicity in the big brown eyes, a charm about the piquantly irregular features and tiptilted nose, that etched themselves into his brain.

Again he was aware of self-annoyance that any girl should make such an impression on him. He was no high-school boy or callow sophomore, to be smitten by a strange face and an elusive charm of personality. Yet, as he ate his dinner his idle mind kept visualizing her over and over again.

Tevvis scribbled a memorandum note or two on the back of an envelope, for use in his new book. This slim girl with eyes two sizes too big for her elfin face would serve finely as

heroine for the novel. She was of unusual
type. Saul wished he might have heard her
speak, so that he could fit the voice to the aspect
in drawing her fictional character. Perhaps, on
the way back to his drawing room ———

But he did not see her again, though he
looked at every occupant of every seat in the
car where she had stopped that morning.
Angry at his own feeling of disappointment,
he returned to his drawing room.

The train was due at Palm Beach a little
before seven in the morning. Thence, Saul
was to taxi out to a dock beyond Jupiter,
where Gedge was to be waiting for him in the
light-draught launch Tevvis had chartered for
the season, and was to convoy him to the Laxahatchee and thence upstream to Sea-Dream
House. He must turn in early if he was to
get a decent night's rest.

To while away the hour before bedtime, Saul
picked up the magazine he had left lying open
on the sofa in his drawing room. He had
scrawled his chosen new name, "Garry Keith,"
in large script across the front of the magazine,

for the benefit of anyone who might glance in at the open door while Saul was at dinner. The sight of his alias still gave him a bad-boy thrill.

As he lifted the magazine, he saw lying under it on the sofa an envelope. He had left no envelope there and its presence puzzled him. Then his eyes focused on its neatly business-like superscription:

"Saul Tevvis, Esq., Drawing-room D., Car Talonia. (Personal and Immediate.)"

Tevvis groaned in disgust. This, then, was the result of his elaborate alias and his crafty efforts to hide his personality in that of the mythical artist, Garry Keith! Thanks to his oft-published photograph, no doubt, somebody on board had recognized him and was taking this way of forcing acquaintanceship or of begging an autograph!

Half inclined to tear up the letter unopened, Tevvis changed his mind and vexedly ripped wide the envelope. Apparently his best efforts to escape from the nuisance of receiving mail were all in vain. He could not escape from chronic letter-writers, even under another name and aboard a fast express. Scowling, he began to read the letter. Then his square jaw fell slack. He read and reread, dizzily:

> "SAUL TEVVIS, ESQ., (*or* GARRY KEITH, ESQ., *if it amuses you to call yourself that*):
>
> "*If you are wise and if you want to keep on staying alive—sheer away from Sea-Dream House. The Laxahatchee region is not a healthful place for you. Sea-Dream House is the most unhealthful spot, for you, on the whole stream.*
>
> WELL-WISHER."

The note had none of the deliberate ill-spelling or other crudities of the typical anonymous letter. It was written in a clerkly hand, and not badly phrased. Its stationery was flawless.

Saul looked up blankly from his fourth perusal of the queer little missive. He forced his brain from its dull astonishment to logical thinking. His close-guarded secret was public property, then? His new name was known. His destination was known. So much, his first moment's thought told him. Then he saw the other side of it.

Some one was warning him that danger awaited him at Sea-Dream House and was bidding him keep away from the Laxahatchee on peril of death. Why? The old house had lain tenantless for an incalculably long time. If there was life-and-death trouble lurking there for Saul Tevvis, what was its nature and why should he be warned in this secretly melodramatic way?

Perhaps the whole thing was a hoax, a practical joke some friend was playing on him. Who knew he was changing his name for the winter and that he was going into hiding at Sea-Dream House? Two people only. Gedge and Musgrave Herne. Gedge was notoriously close-mouthed and had proven in twenty-odd years' service that he was as trustworthy as he was surly. He guarded his employer's interests not only loyally, but savagely. No, Gedge could not have blabbed.

As for Herne—he was the most serious-minded of all Tevvis's friends and he was staunchly reliable. He had given Saul his word not to blab, and he had carried on the negotiations with the Florida agents, using only the name of Garry Keith as that of the house's winter tenant. Tevvis had seen all the correspondence. No, Herne would not talk. He could be trusted.

Yet nobody else had been told. And, since neither of these had betrayed the secret, how did an outsider know? The puzzle waxed more and more unsolvable the more Saul pondered it.

To the threat of danger Saul Tevvis gave not a thought. He had proved, in France, and in many a peace-time crisis, that cowardice and even prudence were not traits of his. But, the chance that he might lose his eagerly-anticipated months of utter seclusion and his chance to write the book whose conception gripped him more and more every day—these things worried him past words.

He rang for the porter, and asked if the

negro had been ordered to leave a note in the drawing room for him. With evident sincerity the man disclaimed all knowledge of the matter. Anyone passing, while Saul was at dinner, could of course have stepped unnoticed into the room and could have shoved the note under the magazine. But which of the train's hundred-odd passengers had done it?

Before turning in, Tevvis walked the train from end to end, scanning face after face, for hint of the epistle's author. But the passengers seemed of the customary winter tourist type. None of them was known to him by sight, even as none of them appeared to pay any heed to him as he walked past.

So long did he lie awake in his berth that night that he all but overslept, and he left the train in a scramble at Palm Beach, without his breakfast. Not until he was well on his way, in the drive out to Jupiter, did he remember again the girl he had seen on the train and whose vision had stuck to his mind all the preceding day. Perhaps she, too, had debarked at Palm Beach or perhaps she had gone on to Miami. In either case, there was no likelihood of his seeing her again.

Under the warmth of the Florida sun and in surroundings of eternal summer, his worry of the night before vanished. Once more he was looking forward avidly to his winter of solitary work. If danger should threaten, he could barricade the house with its own rusted iron shutters and could go on writing. If lion-hunters should swarm down upon him from Palm Beach, Gedge could stave them off. Tevvis could remain at his desk, happily invisible.

The taxi drove him to a crazy dock beyond Jupiter. There, in a consumptive little gas-launch, Gedge awaited him. Beside Gedge stood Bunty.

At first glimpse of her adored master the undersized collie whizzed forward, screeching with ecstasy at the reunion. She flung herself wildly upon Tevvis, then ran around him in delirious circles, yelping and whimpering.

Then she subsided in a quiveringly blissful heap at his feet.

Meantime, Gedge touched his cap sulkily to Tevvis and proceeded to transfer Saul's hand-luggage to the launch. Had Tevvis returned after a ten-year absence on the planet Mars, this would have been Gedge's unenthusiastic greeting to the man for whom right blithely he would have died. Gedge did not go in for demonstrativeness.

The luggage was in place and Saul stepped down into the boat. Gedge started the engine and the launch chugged out into the inlet. Then it was that the Englishman remembered something. Digging down into his pocket, he exhumed a dirty twist of paper, which he handed to his employer.

"While I was a-waiting for you," said he, "a coon roustabout comes along and he asks me to give this to Mr. Garry Keith. I asked him who it was from. He said he didn't know. He said a man had gave it to him and that the man had told him to give it to me to give to you. I made so bold as to read it but I couldn't make any sense out of the reading. Maybe *you* can, sir."

Gingerly, Saul was unrolling the soiled twist of cheap paper. It contained but one line, scrawled in an evidently unpracticed hand, wholly different in every way from the note that had lain under the magazine in the train drawing room. The single line read:

"Still time to turn back. Better do it."

Saul Tevvis glanced only once at the unsigned warning. Then he dropped it overside.

"It doesn't make any sense to me, either, Gedge," said he. "How do you like Sea-Dream House?"

He braced himself for the sluggish current of complaint wherewith Gedge was wont to denounce every change from smug routine of place and of action. To his surprise, the old Englishman rubbed his lean chin and answered, grudgingly:

"I ain't saying, sir, but what I kind of like it. I don't know why I should be liking such a place. But I kind of do. It seems to kind of suit me, somehow. I don't know but I'll be pretty near content there. There's worse places. And this Florida is grand for my rheumatics. Yessir, maybe I don't like it so bad as what I like most places. There's the ghosts, of course. But who's afraid of silly ghosts?"

"The—*what?*" demanded Tevvis, struck by the old fellow's matter-of-fact mention of so grisly a theme.

"The ghosts, sir," repeated Gedge. "They're some pesky when a body wants to sleep, just first off. But I got used to 'em in no time."

Tevvis laughed aloud. The servant spoke as if he were describing mosquitoes.

"Do you mean buzzing little things that sting?" he asked. "Because if you do, those aren't ghosts. They're ——"

"Begging your pardon, sir," said Gedge in icy offendedness, "when I say ghosts, I mean ghosts. Not skeeters, nor yet fleas nor gnats. Ghosts."

He relapsed into sullen silence, skillfully guiding the craft toward the very heart of a

mass of trees that reared like a solid green
wall at the end of the inlet. Presently the
hidden mouth of the Laxahatchee River came
into view, narrow and dark under its arching
wall of foliage. Into the twisting stream sped
the launch; leaving behind it the world of
today and the Florida of tourist and realtor.
Thus had flowed the Laxahatchee between its
mud banks and its double wall of tree and
vine in the day when Señor Don Lopez de
Savedra's longboat had made its first exploratory trip upstream.

The river flowed silent and dark. At a
turn, a fat grayish log on the bank resolved
itself into a suddenly-waked alligator, rising
stiffly on its short legs till it seemed to stand
on the tips of its splay toes; then slithering
noiselessly down into the black water. A giant
bird flapped silently across the gap from forest
refuge to forest refuge. A huge bass broke
water with a splash and a tumble of spray.

Palm and swamp maple and a score of other
trees grew flush with the high banks, lush
and luxuriant. Lianas hung from bough to

bough, like pythons. Somewhere in a thicket a gray mocking-bird was singing its heart out. From a white and dead tree cascaded fiery avalanches of scarlet air-plant. And through all and under all and over all brooded the hot hush of the subtropics and the mystery of the forest.

Up and upstream chugged the little launch, negotiating the river's eccentric twists with ease, and dodging the occasional riffles of sand-shoal. Green gloom shrouded the sun's morning glare. The starkly raucous twentieth century seemed to be a million miles behind and a million years away. Here was primal wilderness cleft by primal watercourse. Saul had an uneasy sense of intruding upon another age and another world.

Then, at a new wrench of the stream's course, the light was strong again. On one shore the rank foliage had been cut away. The sunlight flooded a neglected clearing where a knoll arose gently from the river.

On the knoll's crest stood a large house— a house as out of place in this virgin jungle as might be a picture theater in the heart of the Sahara.

It was ornate, massive, arrogantly elaborate of architecture and position. Only a closer look could reveal that time's tireless tooth was gnawing deep into it and had been gnawing thus for more than two hundred years. Savedra had built for the centuries, not merely for the hour. And his work endured, with only external molderings.

"Kind of mildewed outside, you see, sir," commented Gedge, as he warped toward the rotting pier at the lawn-foot. "But the core's sound as a nut. And the few rooms that I've redded up are as tight and cozy as a body'd ask for."

"Good!" approved Saul. "And I see you've been busy on the grounds, too. The lawn isn't nearly as overgrown and disreputable as when I was here before; and that old driveway and the shrubbery paths have been cleared up. They were one mass of tangled vines and bushes when I saw them. You must have worked hard."

"Yes, sir," admitted Gedge, "I sure *have* worked hard, like I always do. Pretty near worked myself sick. But I didn't get to touch any of the outdoors. Everything outside the house is just like I found it."

"Probably I'm mistaken," said Tevvis. "But that's the impression I get. I thought a lot of rubbish and trees and vines had been cleaned out, in the grounds. I suppose my memory has gotten tangled up with my imagination. Sometimes it does. Most likely it's all just as it was when I saw it."

Chapter Three

HE WAS stepping out of the launch and walking warily along the short strip of swaying pier to the lawn-foot. Above and in front of him, there in the hot sunshine, dozed Sea-Dream House. Its entire framework was of antique ship-timbers, mortised and pinned cunningly together, unrottable and mighty. Here was the pick of the timber of twenty tall ships which had sailed the Spanish Main and whose bent wood Savedra had annexed for his palace.

Incongruously stood the battered carved church doors at the front entrance, with a stained-marble Italian summer-house to one side and an overgrown sunken garden to the other. Above the doors glinted the tarnished bronze tablet, pale and greenish now, and with its oxidized black silvern letters still spelling plainly the stolen legend, "SEA-DREAM HOUSE."

On the rambling ground-floor were few doors and fewer partitions. Low archways of polished ship-timber led from one broad room to another. The central downstairs room was on the style of a castle hall, with a gigantic fireplace at one end and with groined windows. On the mantel still stood carved and twisted and wrought candlesticks, a yard high. In the mantel's center was a roundish lump of some black metal resembling iron, a piece the size of a walnut chipped out of and missing from one arc of it.

Off from the hall, close to the front entrance and shut from the intersecting apartments by a curiously painted door, was a Louis XIV reception room, hung in mildewed tapestries and with wall panelings of yellowed ivory whereon cherubs and flowers and birds had been painted. A few faded-upholstery chairs, once gilt of frame, stood mournfully here and there.

The handle of every door was jet black,

covered carefully with paint. Tevvis wondered at this odd form of decoration until he dug his nail through a bit of the paint. It scaled off in his hand, revealing the solid silver it had been designed to hide from looters. Cunningly adorned but massive iron shutters hung from every blank-faced window—shutters whose barring could turn the lower floor into a fort with masked musketry loopholes.

In the main hall stood against the walls one or two antique muniment chests, partly full of all manner of stuff—yellowed papers; ancient seals; shards of Babylonian tablets; an illuminated breviary with pages torn out; blackened coins of low denomination and of great age and from various lands; tarnished court-sword hilts; and a multitude of other things which Savedra apparently had thought too good to throw away, yet not worth unpacking. Very evidently, all this litter had been pawed over more than once, for it was lying helter-skelter in the chests.

Upstairs Saul Tevvis made his way, followed by Bunty and by Gedge. A dank smell of dead centuries still pervaded the house, in spite of the thorough and continuous airing given it by Gedge. A large bright room overlooking the river had been cleaned and fitted up for Tevvis. Off it was a circular little room, turret-like, with pierced windows and mosaic-ornamented stone floor. Here were Saul's writing desk and his typewriter and two stiff chairs. Here, as he glanced approvingly about the rounded walls, he decided he could work with no hint of outside distraction. It was an ideal study for a man who does not want his thoughts to be allured by his surroundings.

Off it was a still smaller room which Savedra or one of his household had equipped for a workshop. A broken turning lathe and rusted tools were in its corner. Here, too, stood a green iron box, unlocked and more than half full of iron junk and smashed tools and hinges and bolts and padlocks and similar odds and ends tossed there for possible future use by a craftsman whose bones now were dust.

Everywhere, on both floors, was dusty furniture of a kind to make a collector or other antiquarian commit crime for its possession; but presumably of no value to such crackers and conchs and Seminoles as had invaded the house in quest of salable plunder.

On a shelf in Tevvis's study, among other litter, was a brass saucer of Benares workmanship—far more precious in the seventeenth century than in the twentieth—on which lay a massive ring, of the same general appearance in material as the hunk of metal on the hall mantel. It had an ornamentation, consisting of a raised and sharp five-pointed star where ordinarily a seal or stone might have been expected to adorn it. The ring looked more like a "knuckle-duster" than a finger adornment.

Tevvis made a tour of the whole house, before going back to his room to change into the light outing suit which Gedge laid on the bed for him. Most of the house had been left untouched by the servant, only enough of it being cleaned and renovated to serve as living quarters. The heavy door leading from the raftered kitchen to the cellar was not only locked, but was nailed shut. As there seemed no need for opening up the cellar, Gedge had left it untouched. It was so with others of the shut or nailed-up doors, here and there throughout the house.

Saul spent the rest of the day in exploring the mansion and the tangled and overgrown grounds and in getting his belongings arranged to his liking. Change of air and last night's sleeplessness made him yawn over the book he opened as soon as dinner was cleared away. He went up to bed soon after dark.

The silence around him, broken only by the muffled chuckling of the river's sluggish waters against the rotten pier, lulled him to almost instant slumber. He dropped asleep, still stirred by a boyish feeling of adventure and full of plans to begin work early in the morning on his new novel. Bunty, cuddling down at his feet on the bed, stirred him to half-wakefulness once or twice, as in her dreams she pursued some shadowy rabbit or battled against a marauding dog. Lazily Saul would mutter, "Shut up, Bunty!" when her kickings or grunts roused him. Then he would fall asleep again.

Out of the very depths of dreamland he was hoisted to consciousness, hours later, by a very different sound emanating from the little collie. Bunty was growling softly and deep down in her throat. Saul knew the bobtailed dog was not given to growling, except for good cause. So he sat up in bed. In the heavy gloom of the chamber he could see the collie's head and shaggy shoulders vaguely outlined against the paler dark of the nearest open window.

Bunty was sitting up, ears pricked, every line of her wiry body alert. This was not her home; or if it was, she had not been here long enough to know it as home. Thus, she was not on guard. More than once, at hotels, she had been rebuked by Saul for barking a warning when footsteps came down the corridor past his rooms. She had learned better than to give the alarm in a strange abode. Yet, very evidently, she heard or scented something now which made her uneasy.

Tevvis sat and listened. Still the river was chuckling softly around the pier. There were the subdued night notes, too, of subtropical insect life. Somewhere, a night-feeding fish broke water with a slapping sound. A thunderstorm was in progress, far off to seaward. Almost inaudible thunder-grumbles merged with the river sounds, and there were occasional faint flickers of heat lightning, so dim as scarcely to lessen the blanket of black that enwrapped the world.

But, through the blend of soft night noises, as he listened, Saul began to hear another sound, half-indistinguishable, yet persistent and alien. It was a multiple shuffling, as of many bare feet scuffing warily across grass or mud.

The sound was hard to locate, from within the room. At times it seemed above and at times below the listener; then it would come from just outside his window.

Bunty, like all dogs, had far better sense

of sound direction than had any human. Tevvis strained his eyes toward her half-seen sil-
houetted head, between him and the oblong of
lesser denseness. The growling little dog was
peering toward the window. She was in no
doubt whence came that low disturbing shuffle.

Tevvis got out of bed and groped his way
to the window overlooking the neglected lawn
and the river bank. He leaned out and stared
downward through the impenetrable murk. He
could see nothing. Scarcely could he have
seen his hand in front of his face. But here
the sound was much more audible. Here, too,
it seemed to him unmistakably the stealthy
tiptoeing of many bare feet over non-reverber-
ant surface.

From directly underneath him it came, and
it grew ever less distinguishable as it moved
on toward the river-edge. Perhaps it was only
Saul's imagination that made him think he
heard with it the sibilance of heavy breathing
now and then.

He stood there, wondering if this were
merely a distorted aural effect from the region's

night noises and whether he were a fool to lose sleep by trying to locate it. Then came another shimmer of distant heat lightning from far to eastward. Brief and faint was the lightning flare. Yet for the shortest fraction of a second it illumined the lawn below him with a ghostly dimness instead of the former thick dark.

In that breath of time Saul Tevvis gained a mental impression rather than an actual glimpse—something which registered rather on his brain than on his retina. Then, in a trice, it was gone and the lawn was pitch black again.

The blurred impression Tevvis had received was of a throng of dust-colored men—there seemed to be an incredible number of them —all bent low, as under burdens, and all of them strangely clad—all shuffling fast toward the water.

Bunty had pattered to the window at her master's side. As darkness swallowed the universe again, her low-pitched growls swelled suddenly into a deafening fanfare of challenge barks. She reared herself with her white little forefeet planted on the sill and she sent forth her clangor of barks across the black silences. Her hackles were abristle and her body was vibrant.

Like many another dog man, Saul Tevvis was too sensible to discount a warning from his chum collie. Whether or not his own sleep-bemused brain had erred in fancying it had recorded something unusual on the lawn down there, Bunty's miraculous powers of scent and of hearing left her in no doubt at all.

Tevvis groped his way to the door of his room, stumbling against the unfamiliar furniture and wasting a minute or more in a blind-man's-buff quest for the means of egress. When he had opened the door at last and made his unseeing way out into the upper hall, he had still more ado to find the wide stone flight of winding stairs leading to the floor below.

Thus, by the time he had descended and had found his flashlight on the hall table, minutes had drifted past in the course of his fuming search. More moments were wasted by him in finding how to unfasten the intricate bar-and-lock of the door against which Bunty was leaping and barking.

When at last he swung wide the huge door, the collie darted out ahead of him, growling and barking. He heard her tear across the lawn to the pier, there to come to a baffled halt and to fill the night once more with her barks—this time barks of annoyed disappointment, rather than of challenge or of threat.

The flashlight's white sword-blade swung back and forth athwart the lawn. The neglected greensward was as deserted as mid-ocean. No sign of life could the electric flare pick up, from doorway to water-edge.

Tevvis made his way across the drought-dry grass, at a run, making for the pier. Before he could reach it, he tripped over a snarl of bramble and plunged headlong. He threw out both arms, to recover his balance.

Thereby he saved himself from a fall on his face. But thereby, too, his flashlight bounded from his instinctively-opened fingers and fell to the ground at some distance from him. Saul heard it hit the earth and roll along the sloping bank. The impact broke its bulb. Too sensible to waste time feeling about him in the dark for a light which had gone out of use, he made his way blindly back toward the house.

The last part of this trip was eased for him by the appearance of Gedge in the open doorway, swaying a second flashlight inquiringly over the lawn. Roused by Bunty's barking and by Tevvis's noisy efforts to open the front door, the servant had come downstairs in his abbreviated old-fashioned nightshirt to investigate.

"I thought—I—I thought I saw a lot of queer-dressed men traipsing over the grounds," sheepishly explained Tevvis, in no good humor at all. "I went out to look for them. It must have been my imagination. Nothing there. Smashed my light, too. I'm going to bed again. I'm sorry to have routed you out like this. Bunty made a fool of herself—and a fool of *me*. I——"

"No, sir," denied Gedge, as he shut the front doors after his employer and Bunty, "the collie tyke didn't make a fool of herself this time, whatever she may have made of you. She knows. Critters always knows. She seen and she heard and she smelt what she seen and heard and smelt. A couple of other nights— nights when she was sleeping in my room— she got to growling and barking at 'em."

"At what?" asked Saul, crossly, piqued at the man's loftily smug air.

"At the ghosts, of course, sir," said Gedge, in mild surprise at the question. "The same as you saw tonight. The ghosts of Mr. Save- dra's poor killed laborers. Back and forth and to and fro they keep a-going, night after night, between their work on the house and the piles of building material heaped up on the bank. You saw 'em, you said. Them in their funny furren clothes, all working away with their loads of mortar and timbers and such. I never bothered to get out of my bed to look at 'em. But, both nights that Bunty woke me up I lay and listened to 'em. I could hear 'em, real plain, hulking along the lawn and grunting and panting with their backloads, poor lads!"

"Gedge," grumbled Tevvis, "if you'd had better mental advantages in your youth, you might have been a moron by now, instead of a blithering idiot. I'm going to bed. Ghosts? Rot!"

"Mebbe they've kind of scared you, like," suggested Gedge. "Me, now, I'm no more afraid of ghosts than I'd be afraid of the smoke from my pipe. Having nothing to harm me with, they can't harm me. They're only just smoke. I could walk right through one of 'em. No, sir! Ghosts is the least of my worries. Why, I'd walk right up and pat one of 'em, if it'd pleasure the poor lonesome thing. Mosquitoes, now," he added, with a vicious scratch at his left shin—"mosquitoes is different, the pesky cusses! Back in the old country, we don't have 'em. But ghosts? Who minds ghosts?"

As soon as he had finished his early breakfast of dry toast and coffee and orange juice, next morning, Saul Tevvis went to his circular stone study and set avidly to work on the blocking in of his proposed book. So intent was he on the task and so eagerly did his mind rise to the congenial employment, that he grudged the fifteen minutes he took for lunch. Back he went to his desk as soon as he had eaten; toiling with ardent inspiration on the skeleton synopsis which was to serve as framework for the novel's first draft.

In late afternoon, comfortably tired, he laid aside the close-typed pages, and went out in his hired canoe, for an hour of bass-casting. Downstream he let the light craft float while he cast. Bunty cuddled happily in the bow, delighted as always to go boating with her master. The Laxahatchee is one of Florida's best bass streams and one of the least fished. In the zest of his sport, Tevvis forgot ghost scares and work and everything but the joy of taut line and singing reel.

A tributary of the stream seemed to promise sport, with its deep pools and out-jutting tree roots. Up it he paddled, casting softly, landing two big and bellicose bass.

Dusk was beginning to close in. Presently

it occurred to the man that it was time to retrace his way, if he were to be in time for
dinner and thus avoid Gedge's reproachful
glare at the spoiling of a long-worked-over
meal.

But it is one thing to wander into a tributary of the Laxahatchee and quite another thing
to make one's way out through the bewildering
network of streamlets and confluent back-
waters which turn the riverside hinterland into
an all but impenetrable maze. Many a Laxahatchee tourist has learned this to his cost. Saul
was learning it now. An hour's exploratory
paddling brought him no closer to the main
stream than before. Dark was sifting down
from the skies. Under overhanging trees, surrounding objects were invisible.

Once, as he paddled vainly, Tevvis all but
upset his cranky canoe against the scaly back
of a fat alligator. Again, brushing through
sedge, the hot hiss of a cotton-mouth moccasin
made him sheer away and set Bunty to cowering low in the bottom of the boat. The gallant little collie's one utter dread was snakes,

ever since her own anguished experience with
rattlesnake venom.

Then, coming out of the slank, Saul found
himself at the foot of a patch of pine barren.
Here was promise of higher ground and of
possibly clear walking. He beached the canoe,
and he and Bunty swarmed up the sandy bank.
Here it was much lighter and the going was
easier. Tevvis resolved to leave the canoe and
to make his way on foot in the general direction of the river; thence to walk close to its
banks till he should come to Sea-Dream House.

But a quarter-mile of wandering made him
realize he was more completely lost than before. He stood looking about him to get his
bearings. Then mentally shaping his course,
he moved toward a straight vista among the
pines. The third step brought him over his
boot-tops in a marsh formed by ooze in one
of the jungle's hollows. Out he splashed to
drier ground; then halted, blinking.

Down the vista toward him in the eerie dusk
a glimmering white shape was moving.

It seemed to float, rather than to walk. With

a sharp bark, Bunty dashed forward toward the apparition. But as the collie neared the Shape her bobbed tail began to wag violently. She capered about the snowy figure, which bent to pat the little dog.

Tevvis had gone forward instinctively in the wake of his collie. Now he saw the newcomer was a girl, dressed in white. From her free gait and lithe contour it was evident she was young. But in that elusive gloom her face was little more than a pale blur.

"Please don't be frightened," he began, apologetically, as she started slightly on looking up from her patting of Bunty and saw him, "I'm ——"

"Why should I be frightened?" she asked, with a tinge of amusement in her pleasant voice. "What is there to be frightened about?"

So calmly did she take this meeting with a stranger in the heart of this jungle maze at nightfall, that Saul was ashamed of his own banal reassurance.

"I am lost out here," he went on. "I went

fishing and I got into some kind of labyrinth. Then I tried walking, and I don't seem to find my way any better on foot. Can you tell me how to get back to the river? I am living at Sea-Dream House—in case you know where it is."

"Oh!" she exclaimed, in sudden interest. "From your fishing-rod I thought you were just a camper. I might have known better. You must be Mr. Garry Keith, aren't you? All of us have been so interested in you ever since we heard a real live artist was coming here for the winter. I am Wanda Reeve. My father is the clergyman—the missionary, he calls himself—up at Boulding. I'm on my way back there from the Oren cottage. I carried some things down to Mrs. Oren this afternoon. So you're lost? Everyone is who gets out of touch with the river."

"You don't seem to be," he commented. "You were walking along as steadily as if you were on Fifth Avenue. But if you can direct me how to get back to ——"

"I can do better than that," she assured him. "Let's find your canoe. It can't be far from where the pines begin. Then I'll paddle you to Sea-Dream House, and go on up to Boulding and send your canoe back to you in the morning. It seems to be the only way I can 'direct' you home. You'd certainly be lost again if I pointed out the way to you. Nobody who hasn't lived here always, as I have, could find the way out, in this darkness."

Half an hour later—a half hour of delightfully pleasant chat—the canoe touched at the Dream-House pier. Reluctantly Tevvis stepped out. He had found himself talking with this informally-met forest maiden as if he and she were life-long acquaintances. There was an odd charm to their brief association—a charm bred of the place and the time and the circumstances—a charm which swept away the first stiff stages of friendship as by magic. To her, their meeting seemed as natural as to him it was idyllic.

Before they parted and she turned the canoe

bow into the upstream shadows, it was arranged that Saul should come to Boulding next day; for lunch with Wanda and her father.

He trudged across the lawn to the house, half mesmerized, half vexed. He had planned to meet nobody, to form no acquaintanceships which could interfere with his work. Also, he had told himself that never again should a woman stir his nerves or his imagination. Yet ——

"I thought you was dead, sir," Gedge greeted him, sourly, at the door. "The dinner is, anyhow. Clean spoiled. Lord, sir, but look at them shoes of yours!"

Tevvis glanced down at his thick-mired boots. Then, in the doorway, he kicked them off.

"Go up and get my house shoes," he commanded. "And take these muddy boots with you. I stumbled into a swamp."

He sat down at the foot of the steps to await the servant's return with his footgear. Bunty

stood beside him, gazing in sudden interest up
the winding stairway.

A screech of mortal terror shattered the
house's silences. Down the stairs Gedge flung
himself, leaping rather than running. His face
was ghastly, drawn, agonized. Panic horror
bulged from his eyes. Past the astonished Tevvis he fled unheeding, and rushed out onto
the dark lawn. The iron-nerved manservant
was delirious with fright.

Bunty had been starting excitedly up the
stairs as Gedge all but collided with her in
his flying descent. Now she galloped up,
growling savagely. As Tevvis made as though
to follow her, she shrieked loudly in fear, from
somewhere in the darkness of the second floor.
Then down the stairs she catapulted, and
flashed across the hall and through the half-
shut front door whence Gedge had escaped
into the night. Eerily the door clanged shut
behind her.

Saul Tevvis was left standing bewildered,
stark alone, in the sinister house whence his

two wontedly fearless comrades had rushed in blind panic.

Slowly, with shoulders squared, he prepared to mount the stairs toward the terror-charged blackness of the floor above.

Chapter Four

SAUL TEVVIS stood, peering up the stairway into the blackness above. The thud of Gedge's fleeing feet and of Bunty's pattering flight across the lawn had died on his ears. The house was deathly silent; the stillness pressing in, painfully, on the ears of the listening man.

Then, setting his teeth and forcing back the wondering horror that encompassed his nerves and heart at the panic rout of the dog and the servant, he made his way resolutely up the ever-darker stairs.

Up there, somewhere in the mystic shadows, lurked a Thing so horrifying as to make gallant little Bunty scamper yelling from the house, with no thought for the safety of the master she worshiped. She had deserted him.

Up there, somewhere, lurked a Thing so horrifying as to make plucky old Gedge go screeching past Tevvis and out into the night, in a delirium of terror—Gedge who, as a mere boy, had won the Victoria Cross for reckless contempt of danger, and who knew not the meaning of fear.

Saul was left alone to face the Thing; whatever it might be.

Steeling himself for the encounter and tensing his compactly powerful muscles, he mounted the stone steps toward the second floor. As he went he picked up one of the flashlights from the table in the hall.

A white sweep of radiance from the light preceded him as he reached the landing above. It played inquiringly along the upper hall, peeping into cranny and corner and niche. It cast an illumination that routed the wavering shadows and made the track of its rays as bright as daylight.

From room to room Tevvis hurried, ever heralded by the glare of his electric torch. Nothing stirred. No hideous Shape darted forth from the darkness to impart to him the wild fright which had obsessed Gedge and the collie.

His taut nerves began to relax. There was an element of the absurd in his bracing himself to face a Thing of stark frightfulness, and then in his finding only the familiar objects of the ancient house. Back and forth through the second floor he roamed, lighting lamps as he went. All was peaceful, if gloomy.

At last, in self-disgust at his own useless heroics and in stronger scorn for the cowardly servant and dog, he retraced his steps down the winding stone stairway to the main hall. As he did so he saw one half of the carved front doors begin to swing silently open, inch by inch.

Then, through the slit and framed against the outer darkness appeared a dimly seen white face.

Tevvis strode forward angrily. As he approached, the door swung wide, at a brisker speed, and Gedge sidled shamefacedly into the room. At his heels trotted Bunty, still cowed, but seeming vastly ashamed of having deserted her master.

"Too bad we haven't a phonograph with a 'Hail, the Conquering Hero Comes' record on it, for me to play in your honor, Gedge!" remarked Tevvis. "By the way, when you won that Victoria Cross of yours, was it for your sublime speed in outrunning the pursuing enemy? Or were you so scared, for once, that you couldn't run, and they thought you stood your ground out of courage? For a man of your age, you certainly have a talented pair of legs and super-shriek-power lungs."

"Yessir," assented Gedge, standing stiffly at attention, the ghastly white of fear changing slowly in his wooden face to a purplish-scarlet flush of shame at his employer's tongue-lashing. "Yessir. Keep on a-bawling me out, sir. I got it coming to me. I deserve it. I'm a yellow old coward, sir."

"You're all that," answered Saul, still ruffled of temper and of nerve. "But it's a point in your favor that you admit it. I'm worse ashamed of Bunty, here, than I am of you.

She's a collie.   And collies are supposed to die for the humans they serve; not to run ki-yi-ing from the first danger.   No, old girl," as Bunty, at sound of her name, sniffed timidly at his hand and made as though to cuddle up to him. "Keep out of my way!   You're as yellow as your coat, and not half as clean.   Go over there and lie down.   Next time I'm looking for a trusty protector, I'll buy a nice valorous mouse instead of a collie.   You're a coward, Bunty. A sneaking mutt!"

"Excusing me for speaking out of turn, sir," interposed Gedge, hotly, as the sensitive collie shrank away from the scoffing rebuke in Tevvis's loved voice, "but you got no call to say them things about the good little dog.   She ain't afraid of anything that's flesh and blood; and you can't say she is.   When she nailed that sneak thief in your rooms, last year, she got to his throat and she held him, even after he'd bust in two of her ribs with his kicks and knifed her in the side.   And she kept my head above the water, that time I got the cramps in Great South Bay; even when it pretty near drowned her to do it. She was about dead when you hauled the two of us ashore. But she wouldn't give up. And you saw her tackle that big she police dog, more'n double her size, and kill the big brute in square fight. Nope, Bunty ain't yellow, even if I am. And the two of us never yet turned tail on anything human, nor yet we never won't. When it comes to ghosts, that's something else."

He subsided into glumly sheepish silence, furtively reaching out to give the cringing Bunty a reassuring pat on her trembling head. Tevvis glowered doubtfully at the two renegades, his own wrath ebbing.

"Ghosts?" he snorted. "Ghosts, again, eh? That was what you ran away from is it, Gedge —you who aren't afraid of a ghost? Weren't you saying, last night, that ghosts can't harm anyone? Weren't you saying you'd like to pat one of them? Then ——"

"Yessir, I was," replied Gedge. "But when it comes to TWO ghosts—both of 'em glowing-like with the fire of the Pit itself—and when they're fighting, up yonder, like a brace of devils—and when one of 'em sinks clean through a solid stone floor and t'other fades through a solid wall—all in the second or so that I'm gowking at 'em ——"

"Quite!" agreed Tevvis, drily, cutting in on the blithered narrative. "Quite so. A very pretty ghost story as it stands, Gedge. I wouldn't try to improve on it if I were you, or embellish it any more. Imaginative fiction isn't your forte. You do it rather badly. Suppose we let it go at that."

"You—you don't believe me, sir?" stammered Gedge.

"Frankly, I don't. I've seldom heard a sillier lie. Two demons, tastefully clad in the flames of the Pit, are having a fine death-grapple in the upper hallway, and at sight of you they fade through stone and wood. All this goes on while I'm standing down here, within thirty feet of it, and I don't hear or see a thing. No, Gedge; next time take a little longer and think up a better one. It won't wash."

"You don't think I saw anything up there, sir?" babbled the scared old man. "You think ——?"

"I know very well you saw something up there, or else something terrifying happened to you," answered Tevvis. "Nobody who saw your face or heard your unearthly yell, as you sprinted downstairs, could doubt that. What it was you really saw or what it was that happened to you, I don't know; and you seem to have made up your mind not to tell. So you invent this sweet yarn about fiery ghosts. Never mind! If you won't tell, you won't; and I'm not going to waste breath in coaxing you to. But cut out that silly ghost-fight yarn. As a fiction writer, it offends my common sense. Now go out to the kitchen and rustle me some dinner. I won't test your shaky heroism by telling you to go upstairs again for my house shoes. I'll brave the warring fire-ghosts by finding those for myself. But get me some dinner. I'm half starved."

Saul Tevvis's nerves and temper, as a rule, were on a par with the trained physical strength of his muscularly thickset body. But temper and nerves were wrenched by the last few minutes' events; the more so because he was convinced that Gedge was lying to him and because he did not care for mysteries outside the covers of a novel.

Then, as Gedge departed humbly on his errand of dinner-getting, Saul's gaze turned in perplexity, toward Bunty. A sight which might scare the unimaginative old manservant would not be likely to have the same effect on the fiery little collie. Yet, even now she was trembling slightly as she slunk to and fro. Flecks of foam spattered her nervously panting jaws. Appealingly her deep-set dark eyes were fixed on the master whose reproof had shamed her.

Tevvis snapped his fingers invitingly. With a bound the dog was at his side, pressing close against him, whimpering and rubbing her head against his knee, eager to make up and to be forgiven. Absently Saul stroked the silken head, speaking reassuringly to the collie.

"It's all right, old girl!" he soothed her;

adding, under his breath, "but I wish you could talk. *You'd* tell me what really happened upstairs, there. You wouldn't tell me a clumsy lie, like old Gedge. Listen, girl. I'm going up there, now, to get my shoes. I want you to come along. If you don't, you'll always be scared of that floor. Come."

With no hesitance at all Bunty followed him, even pushing past him on the stairway and preceding him along the hallway to his bedroom. Whatever had made her bolt yelping out into the night, it was evident she felt no present terror of the scene of her panic.

Saul slept troubledly, and awoke early. Long he lay in bed, looking out into the sunrise. Usually he woke clear-brained and energetic. This morning a tired lassitude possessed him. Strangely enough, his thoughts were not of the last evening's queer happenings, but played perplexingly about the memory of the white-clad girl of the jungle-vista.

He found himself looking forward with real anticipation to his luncheon with her and her father at Boulding. He fell to remembering details of her free forest gait, her lithe figure, the turn of her head, and he tried to visualize the face which twilight had made only a delicate blur to his peering eyes.

Then he berated himself soundly for his silly mental maunderings. He had left New York partly to escape from an off-chance of being caught again in a miserable net of infatuation by Barbara Crale. He had sworn to himself that never again would he undergo the tortures a worthless woman can inflict on a fool who loves her. Henceforth, women were to be as mere lay figures to him, or, at most, amusing dinner- or tea-table companions.

Yet, at the very outset of his exile he had chanced to see a girl on the train who had filled his mind and his imagination, despite his best efforts to banish her from his thoughts. And now, a bare two days later, he had seen dimly in the dusk another girl, whose very face he could not discern and with whom he had chatted with odd freedom for perhaps half an hour.

And she was filling his memory and his rebellious fancy! Was his mind collapsing, that he brooded like a lovesick schoolboy on every woman he happened to see? If so, it was high time he buried himself in his work and gave his brain a saner and more profitable outlet for its energies.

As to this luncheon at Boulding, with the forest-maid and her missionary father—well, he would send Gedge upstream with a stiffly civil note of regret, saying Mr. Garry Keith would be too busy to keep the engagement. Then he would settle down to a real day's work.

He got up and bathed and shaved, then reached for the shabby outing suit he had worn on the preceding day. But, after a glance at it, he turned to his wardrobe closet and took therefrom a blue serge reefer coat and a pair of unworn white flannel trousers and white buckskin shoes. Carefully did he ponder the choice of silk shirt and tie. For a man who planned to spend the whole day at his desk, he arrayed himself in unwonted splendor.

As he munched the breakfast prepared by the still humiliated Gedge, he told himself it would not be necessary to send a note to Wanda Reeve; for she had spoken of bringing the canoe back to Sea-Dream House pier sometime during the morning. He could tell her then that he would be too busy to accept her invitation, and he could word his regrets in such way as to let her see he desired to be let alone during the rest of his stay on the Laxahatchee. That was the only possible way to get his work done.

Better still, the day promised to be hot. Perhaps Wanda would send the canoe back to him by some negro boy, instead of paddling all the way downstream herself. That was likely, since there was luncheon for her to supervise or prepare. So, it might be better to save her the trouble and expense of hiring a boy to bring it downstream by going himself to Boulding in his launch, and towing the canoe back to the pier. Yes, that would be much better.

The canoe would be beached at Boulding; and he could step ashore and leave word at Wanda's home that he could not lunch with her and her father. He might even stop a few minutes to meet Mr. Reeve and to chat with the girl herself. Surely that would be more civil than to send her a curt note.

After all, she had saved him from a night of lost wandering in that mosquito-cursed backwater jungle. He owed her a certain meed of courtesy for that. Perhaps it might be better if he should sacrifice this one half-day's work and lunch at the parsonage with her. Probably she had put herself out to make more or less elaborate preparations for his coming. During the meal he could explain tactfully that he would not have time to call again.

To Gedge's astonishment, Saul Tevvis set down his half-emptied coffee cup and broke into a shout of laughter.

"I called you a coward, last night," Saul

explained, when he could control his voice, "and you're not a coward. But you or anyone else can call me a hypocrite and be dead right. That's what I am, Gedge—the worst kind of hypocrite—the kind that deceives himself. And I never knew it till this minute. Funny, isn't it?"

"I've heard funnier things," sniffed Gedge, as ever on the glum defensive in the presence of a joke he could not understand. "Mebbe I've heard as many as seven or nine funnier things—in music halls, back home, or at vawd-vil shows in New York. Not but what I'm glad to hear you laugh again, sir. I'm feeling some gay myself, this morning. I don't know what there is about this queer place that makes me come pretty near to liking it, ghosts and all. It don't make sense I should like it down here. But I kind of do, somehow or other. Mebbe ancestors of mine was pirates or something."

"Perhaps it reminds you of Mile End Road," suggested Tevvis, solemnly.

"No, sir, I think not, sir," denied Gedge,

with entire sincerity. "In fact, it don't hardly remind me of Mile End Road at all, sir. Not even of ——"

"Perhaps not," conceded Tevvis, adding: "I shan't be home for lunch. I'm going up to Boulding in the motor-boat. I'll be back early and try to get some work done."

Upstream he guided the launch, with some difficulty making the many twists and turns and avoiding shoals and projecting dead logs. The narrow black river was gay in the morning sunlight, and athrill with insect life. Mocking-birds sang overhead. Here and there a giant crane would flap across the water, with long legs atrail.

In another twenty minutes or less the boat emerged into somewhat wider water. Here on one side of the bank for perhaps half a mile the foliage had been cleared away. A sandy stretch of land arose to the right, with a line of decayed little docks fringing it. Beyond, a straggling cracker village ran inland.

For the most part, the houses were mere

cabins, with patches of truck garden around and behind them and with rickety picket fences shutting them off from the single unpaved winding street. At the townlet's center arose the short white steeple of a clapboarded little church. On either side of the church was a house larger and more pretentious than the surrounding cabins.

Each of these two better houses was set in its own well-kept grounds. One of them, unquestionably, must be the parsonage, Wanda Reeve's home.

Amid a huddle of more or less disreputable boats at the docks, Tevvis's canoe was moored. Saul fastened his motor-boat alongside it and made his way up the sandy street toward the church. As he went he wondered which of the two larger houses was the parsonage. Then he decided it must be the one on the church's hither side, as this was not only nearer to the churchyard itself, but was of a sprucer aspect and was better built than was the house on the far side.

Accordingly, he turned in at the gate and walked up a shell-path between rows of small box-trees, to the front porch. There was no name plate. He smiled at his own folly in looking for one in this region where doubtless everyone knew where everyone else lived.

He tapped with the brass door-knocker, then, receiving no answer, he rapped again and more loudly. Light footsteps sounded in the inner hallway, and the door was opened.

Standing inquiringly on the threshold was a man in immaculate cream-colored silk pongee. He was tall and lean and dark, high of cheek-bones and aquiline of nose. There was a faintly coppery tinge to his high-bred face. Apparently he had a strong admixture of Indian blood. Hanging over one arm was a much-spotted laboratory apron which he seemed to have discarded as he came to the door.

"Is this the Reverend Mr. Reeves?" asked Tevvis, wondering if Wanda was as much like an Indian, in looks, as was this aristocratic-looking man who seemed far too young to be her father.

"No," answered the pongee-clad host. "He lives just the other side of the church. Most strangers mistake this house for the parsonage, for some reason. Aren't you Mr. Garry Keith?" he continued, holding out his slender hand in greeting.

"Yes," replied Tevvis, taking the outstretched hand. "But I'm sure I haven't met you before. If I have, forgive me for being so rude as to forget it. I——"

"No, we haven't met anywhere," the other reassured him, pleasantly, "so you haven't been rude. But all of us have been interested in you, ever since we found we were to have a New York painter for our neighbor. So I jumped to conclusions. I am John King. Won't you come in for a few minutes, if you aren't in a hurry?"

There was much graciousness in voice and gesture and smile, as King stood aside for his guest to enter the cool hallway. The man seemed to take his invitation's acceptance for granted.

Saul found himself, with no special volition of his own, stepping into the house of this stranger whose courtesy had such a compelling note in it and whose coal-black eyes seemed to be reading him to the heart.

The hall and the rooms leading out from it were pleasantly furnished and with much taste. There was no sign of the poverty or of the tawdriness which might have been expected in such a region.

King ushered his guest into a dim-lit study and motioned him toward one of its deep leather chairs. Above the stone mantel hung a complete Indian warrior costume, with its weapons and accouterments fastened neatly just beneath.

"A fine trophy you have there," commented Tevvis, eyeing with approval the striking outfit. "One of the best I have seen this side of the Smithsonian. It ——"

"That is not a trophy," King corrected him, holding forth a box of cigars to the guest. "That is my own war dress. As you have seen, I am an Indian. That is the equipment and clothing of a Seminole war chief. It is my right, and my pleasure, to keep it here on my walls even though it is as useless and as out-of-date as its own tomahawk."

Chapter Five

THERE was a shade of sadness in King's deep voice. Tevvis felt vaguely embarrassed at his own patronizing comment on the costume.

"Yes," he said, "I inferred you had Indian blood. And, as you are in southern Florida, I might have guessed you are a Seminole. But ——"

"But you are wondering, in the back of your mind," suggested King, "why I am not living in a tepee and wearing a blanket and grunting 'How!' at you."

"No, no!" disclaimed Tevvis. "I ——"

"Yes, yes," laughingly persisted King. "Everyone whom I meet for the first time seems to be wondering that. Back during my college days I was on vacation down near Long Key, on a fishing trip. A tourist came up to me

there and asked me, 'Big Injun ever hear of
Great White Father up at Washington?' "

"No!" cried Saul, incredulous.

"I was in khaki, torn khaki at that. We'd
been fishing out on the reef for two days. I
couldn't blame the fellow. So I just answered, 'If you mean have I heard of President
Taft, he and I are members of the same fra-
ternity at college and I had the pleasure of
lunching with him last week."

"Good!" applauded Tevvis.

"You see," went on King, "many of my
people made fortunes in the sale of their Everglades lands. My father, their chief, made,
of course, more than any of the rest. He
sent me to college, and then to Oxford for a
year to study chemistry. That has always
been my fad—as you may have guessed from
the acid-spotted apron I was carrying when
your knock brought me out from my lab. My
father built this house on the site of his ancestors' biggest village and on the very spot
where their longhouse stood. I spend most
of my time down here. It is a pleasant enough

life for a lonely man with a hobby. An educated Indian must always be lonely. And my radium experiments are enough to keep me interested. Radium and its by-products are fascinating."

"I dabbled with it a bit in my senior year at Dartmouth," said Tevvis, keenly interested, "and I went into it just enough to know nothing, but to want to know much. Sometime may I look at your lab?"

By way of answer, King led the way to an adjoining room which jutted out into the garden. Here, between shiningly white tiled walls and on polished flooring, was set up a comprehensive, if compact laboratory, as out of place in this wilderness hinterland as was Sea-Dream House itself. Tevvis glanced about him in genuine admiration, noting and classifying the few articles with which his own college laboratory work had made him familiar.

"I have been playing, rather than working, lately," explained King. "I have become fascinated with what old Carrick, at Oxford, used to call 'the toyland of chemistry.' Know much about radiolite?"

"Almost nothing," confessed Saul, "except it's the stuff they use to illumine watch dials. But we hardly touched on it in the little dabbling I did at college. Is that what you are 'playing' with, nowadays?"

"Yes," said King, "when I ought to be trying to accomplish something seriously worth while."

"Can I see some of your work—or your play, as you call it?"

"Here is a simple little experiment that may amuse you," returned King, darkening the room by pulling down its thick black window curtains; then moving over to a wall cabinet and taking from it an oval glass container with protuberances sticking out here and there from it. "This is a 'beaker,' as your own lab work tells you. It seems empty and the glass looks dirty in spots. Well, this beaker contains radium."

"But ——"

"I know there are tiny particles of radium

in it, because, long ago, over at Oxford, it contained radium. It is still there, even though we can't see it. Here is a common nail file. Watch me scrape this 'empty' beaker with it. I'll scrape it all around the sides. That will make some of the particles of invisible radium stick to the file point. Now, to make the invisible become visible!" he continued, turning to the table and picking up a magnifying glass.

"Look!" directed King. "Now when I hold this file above the zinc-sulphide screen, you can see glowing spots—'alpha rays,' we call them —shooting off the file tip, like so many tiny lightning bolts. They shoot off the tip and hit the screen. Pretty, isn't it?"

"Pretty?" repeated Tevvis, peering interestedly through the glass. "It's wonderful. I ——"

"No," denied King, tolerantly, "but here is something that *is* 'wonderful.' If I were to sit here like this for the rest of my life, I could still watch that infinitesimal particle of radium shoot off sparks from the file tip to the screen. At my death, a child could take the file from my hand and go on watching that shower of miniature thunderbolts till he was an old man; and his grandchildren could do the same, for centuries. All from that one speck of radium that is too small for the human eye to see.

"At the end of about seventeen hundred years the size of that speck of radium would have diminished by perhaps one-half, in spite of all the trillions of sparks it would have been shooting forth for nearly eighteen centuries. That is the basis of my radiolite experiments. If you look at a watch dial's illumination, you see only a dull glow. Look at it through a strong enough glass and you'll see this same bombardment of fire-sparks. But I'm boring you," he interrupted himself. "Besides, the results of my own private experiments haven't reached the 'show-off' stage yet."

Ignoring Saul's eager disclaimers, he flooded the room with sunlight again, then put aside his simple apparatus and led the way back to the study.

"Sometime, when my present experiments are farther advanced," said he, "won't you come over here again and watch me putter around with them?"

"Indeed I shall!" promised Saul, realizing the loneliness of mind and of scientific interest that must be King's, in the midst of this ignorant neighborhood. "You can't keep me away. And I wish you'd drop down on me sometimes at Sea-Dream House. We are near neighbors, you know."

Instantly he regretted giving the politely necessary invitation. Twenty-four hours earlier he had been blissfully free from possible interruptions to his cherished work. Now, in that space of time, he had formed two acquaintanceships.

He had just asked John King to his house. He must return in some way the luncheon at the parsonage. That meant King and Wanda and Mr. Reeve would all have the right to break in on his writing hours. Truly, a wilderness was not so satisfactorily lonely as he had dreamed it must be!

"I shall be gladder to call on you than you realize," King was saying, with sudden enthusiasm. "You see, your house has always held tremendous interest for me. Once, as a little boy, I broke in there, and I had a beautiful time wandering spookily around, fingering everything and reconstructing its past. I told my father where I had been. He horsewhipped me. Then he read me a stern lecture on the mortal sin of trespass and of rude curiosity. (For those *are* sins, to my race, you know.) And he made me give solemn promise never to trespass there again. But it can hardly be called trespass or a breaking of my vow, to go there on your invitation. So I accept, most eagerly, before you can reconsider. And I warn you I shall ask leave to wander all over the house again, if I may."

"Indeed you may!" assented Tevvis. "In fact, I wish you would. Because, having lived down here always, you may be able to tell me a number of things about it that I am curious to hear. I know only the bare outline—the tale of Señor Don Lopez de Savedra's dream of a palace in the jungle, and his making the dream come true by the help of the Seminole chief, Laxahatchee, and then the yarn that he got rid of Laxahatchee ———"

"My ancestor," supplemented John King, speaking with a tinge of reverence.

"Oh, I beg your pardon a thousand times!" exclaimed Tevvis, in contrition at his own flippant tone in speaking of the long-dead chief.

"You needn't feel uncomfortable about it," King reassured him, smiling. "Of course, you didn't know. And even if you had known, neither you nor any other white man could have understood what a hallowed Memory a mighty chief and medicine-man like Laxahatchee is to his descendants and his tribesfolk. To us, our greatest chiefs of past days are as demi-gods to be all but worshiped. And Laxahatchee was the greatest of them all. His death was a blow that checked the fast-growing power and future of the whole Seminole nation."

"I didn't know ——" stammered Saul, in dire contrition at his own unwitting rudeness.

"He and his predecessors had built up and developed and strengthened my people," pursued King. "Perhaps there were no heights they might not have reached if Laxahatchee had lived to put his genius-plans into effect and to pass them on to his son. As it is, we are the only Indian people the United States never wholly conquered. There is that to remember with some slight pride. And to this day there is no pauper and no criminal among us. What might we not have grown to be if ——"

He checked his fast-spoken harangue, laughed and said: "It is I who must apologize, this time, for making you listen to the futile brag of a tribeless chief who tries for the most part to keep his mind in the normal twentieth century. Yes, it is true, Laxahatchee was done to death by Savedra. Where and how, nobody knows. My people have handed down a rumor that Savedra concealed his body in one of the odd hiding-places he had the foreign architect devise so cunningly in his house. Now, perhaps you can see why my gentle father lost control of himself and beat me when he found I had been prowling through that house from mischievous curiosity, and why he made me swear never to trespass there again. And you can see why I am eager to go through it sometime."

"Indeed I can!" cried Saul, strangely moved. "And I beg you will come there often and explore it from top to bottom. It is yours, to wander about in and to examine to your heart's content. Please remember that. I mean it. I can understand what memories lie hidden there for you, Mr. King. By the way, 'King' can't very well be your native name, can it? If ——"

"It is the name my father took when he was educated at Carlisle," said the Seminole. "His own long tribal name was rough on white men's tongues. So he used his title as his name. For the Seminole sachems were kings, rather than mere chiefs. He called himself 'King.' 'John King.' And he passed his name down to me."

"I see," said Tevvis, lamely, tingling with reluctant sympathy and liking for this last descendant of a mighty line of rulers and for his present aloneness. "And ——"

"By the way," commented King, with abrupt change of subject, "will you forgive my rudeness if I say what no doubt many other people have said to you during the past few months? You look enough like this new literary genius, Saul Tevvis, to be his brother. I saw a rotogravure picture of him in one of the Sunday papers last week and I studied it with special interest because I had just finished reading his book, *Ropes of Sand*. The resemblance is startling."

"So I've heard," replied Saul, newly uncomfortable at his chosen alias. "Several people say I look like him."

He got to his feet, holding out his hand in farewell.

"I must go on to the parsonage," said he.

"Thanks for a mighty interesting half-hour. Yesterday afternoon I got lost in that maze of backwater behind the river. Miss Wanda Reeve found me and brought me back home. She was good enough to ask me to lunch with her and her father. I ——"

The Indian's sensitively stolid face changed ever so slightly. Then he answered:

"I am glad you have met the only worthwhile people in the neighborhood, so soon. You will like Mr. Reeve. He is doing a wonderful missionary work among the back-country crackers and among scattered families of my own people. Without him and his daughter for close neighbors, I might not be able to endure life down here. . . . In your inspections of Sea-Dream House, have you happened to notice the big lump of metal that stood on the mantel in the main hall the time I trespassed there?"

"Yes," said Tevvis, curiously, "and I wondered if it was a cannon-ball from one of Savedra's pirate ships."

"No," responded King. "It is a meteorite.

It fell in the very middle of the lawn, the night Savedra took possession there. Laxahatchee told him it was an omen and advised him to leave it alone. But Savedra had it dug up. He bragged: 'This is a chunk of pig-iron, but it was smelted in the Fires of the Stars!' A lump broke loose from it. Savedra had his ironworker make it into a ring, with the five-starred emblem of his family standing out from it. There is some story—I don't know what—about a curse that goes with the ring. Whatever the legend may be, it has been potent enough to keep any sneak thief from stealing the ugly thing. At least, the ring was still there, in a little brass dish, when I made my memorable tour of Sea-Dream House as a youngster. Perhaps——"

"It's still there," said Tevvis. "I saw it as soon as I got to the house, and I wondered about it. I shall be more interested in the meteorite itself, now you've told me what it is. I was going to have it flung into the river as junk. . . . Come and see me."

He left his pongee-clad host in the doorway,

and he made his own way, under the increasingly hot sun, past the church and to the house just beyond it.

A grizzled man with stooped shoulders was writing on the hibiscus-flaming little front porch as Saul came up the walk. The man got to his feet and came forward courteously to welcome his guest.

"Mr. Garry Keith?" he asked, shaking hands with much cordiality. "I'm Malcolm Reeve. My daughter told me of having the pleasure of meeting you, and she told me we are to have you here for lunch today. I am more glad than I can tell you. Here in this solitary tract a new neighbor or guest is a boon. Wanda is working in her garden. Shall I take you to her?"

He led the way around the porch, toward a stretch of shining back garden at whose farther end a slender figure was bending above some newly-transplanted roses.

"Dear!" called the clergyman, "Mr. Keith is here. I'm sending him out to you."

Evidently relieved at the early chance to

get back to his interrupted sermon-writing, Mr. Reeve returned to the front porch, leaving Tevvis to find his way down the winding garden path to the girl who came eagerly to meet him.

The sun made radiant her face as she advanced. On it was the surprised happiness of a child whose loved playmate has come for a visit. But Saul Tevvis gave only passing heed to her happy expression.

He was blinking in amaze at her. Here was not only the forest-maid of the dusky evening before; but here was also the girl he had seen on the southbound train, the girl whose features and expression he had been unable to banish from his memory. Now he understood why the two presumably different girls had made the same odd impression on him in such brief space of time.

In another moment Tevvis and Wanda were face to face under the revealing glare of the subtropic sun and their eyes met.

Instantly the girl's gladly eager expression underwent a ludicrously swift change. Her face flushed hotly, then went pallid, as her dark eyes focused in sudden astonishment on the man's visage. The merrily soft brown eyes hardened and froze. The dainty little features set into an aspect of unmasked hostility. She stood stockstill, and stared up at him with that newly wrathful gaze.

Ignoring Saul's eagerly outthrust hand, she bowed stiffly, almost imperceptibly.

"I am sorry," she said, her sweet voice as icy as her eyes, "but I find my father and I have an engagement for this noon that we cannot easily break. So we must deny ourselves the pleasure of having you lunch with us."

He stood staring, bewildered. Her swift change of manner left him momentarily wordless. He could not understand it. The prim diction was backed by cold distaste of manner and of expression.

"I am sorry," she said again, adding: "You will find your canoe at the docks. I meant to send it down earlier."

Still he stood agape. To his mind came Mr. Reeve's words, "She told me we are to have you here for lunch today." That had been barely two minutes earlier. Reeve had said nothing of another engagement which must banish the luncheon. And at her father's calling of the name "Keith" her eyes had lighted as if from some inner sunray. Only when she saw fully his face did she freeze into icy hostility. It did not make sense to the man.

"I have just finished my gardening," she went on, presently, in the same chilledly civil voice, "and I have important letters to write for my father—letters that must go down to Jupiter in time for the afternoon mail. I am sure you will excuse me if I ———"

"Certainly," he made shift to mumble, trying to rally from the shock of her unfriendly manner. "And forgive me for intruding on a busy morning. I am sorry to have made myself unwelcome. I ———"

His words trailed away to an embarrassed silence as he saw his ignored hand was still foolishly outstretched toward her. She glanced down at it impersonally, as at some specimen in which she felt no interest.

Saul Tevvis let the hand sag back to his side. Bowing, he turned away, moving dazedly up the garden path toward the side gate and out of it into the sandy by-road. Half blindly he began to retrace his steps toward the docks.

His mind was full of perplexed hurt. He had not said or done anything to offend this capricious girl who had taken such illogical hold upon his imagination and heart. He had said or done nothing to warrant her in freezing him or in virtually ordering him from her home. Aware of his own innocence in the matter, he could not well have asked her for an explanation.

Rolling the puzzling topic over and over in his bemused mind, the only solution he could arrive at was that, by daylight, his face or his personality had proven actively unpleasant to her and that she had lacked the breeding or the tact to hide her repulsion. Yet she did not seem ill-bred, or lacking in knowledge of social decencies.

It was a vexing mystery. It was more. It was a genuine hurt. With amazement, Tevvis realized how strong a hold she had taken upon him during their sketchily short meetings. Well, it would serve one good purpose, at least—it would free him from interruptions in his work. This consoling thought failed to console. Saul Tevvis began to hate his work.

As he passed John King's house, the Seminole was standing at the gate.

"I'm going to start in begging neighborly favors at once, Mr. Keith," said King. "I have to go downstream to Shuflin's. One of my boats is covered with wet paint, and the other has sprung a leak and my canoe was stove in by a drifting log yesterday. May I ask you for a lift as far as Sea-Dream House? I can make my way afoot, from there, over the trails."

"You can do better," answered Saul, queerly glad of a friendly word after Wanda's stoniness toward him. "Come down to Sea-Dream House with me and then take my canoe for the rest of the trip. You can send it back this evening or tomorrow."

Together they walked down the hot road to the landing, and fastened the canoe to the launch's stern by the painter, then boarded the launch and set forth. John King talked well and gayly, of the region and its oddities. As they neared the Sea-Dream House pier, he asked:

"You've heard all the myriad ghost stories, of course, that are draped about your new home? I never knew of any one house so completely outfitted with spook yarns. There are enough of them to furnish a whole haunted village. Savedra's murdered workmen parading the grounds, for instance; and Savedra and my great ancestor grappling in phantom conflict on the scene of their real-life struggle, and the slain architect coming back to tug with ghostly fingers at the stones and timbers of the house in an attempt to spite Savedra's ghost by tearing it down. I could tell you such stories by the hour, all of them splendidly authentic and splendidly impossible."

He paused. Through his carelessness of manner he seemed to be waiting with some interest for Saul's reply. It was on the tip of Tevvis's tongue to tell about his own blurred vision of the strangely-dressed and burden-bent men on the lawn and of his servant's weird account of the two fiery ghosts battling in the upper hallway.

But, manlike, he feared derision by seeming to believe such asinine tales or even by repeating them with a possible semblance of belief to this grave-faced guest of his. So he looked politely interested and made no reply, but busied himself in steering around a difficult bend in the river and in swinging the trailed canoe out far enough to avoid the shelving bank.

Chapter Six

JOHN KING waited for an instant; then, with a deprecatory smile, he went on:

"Such stories gather around every empty house in an unsettled place like this. But there is more groundwork for these than for most inventions of the kind. You see, Mr. Keith, this is a strange backwater of civilization. That means it has its quota of moonshiners and, of recent years, bootleggers as well. Probably some bootleg crew may have used the house or its cellars to hide liquor in, on the way from the West Indies, or some moonshine gang may have relied on its remoteness to plant a still there or to store illicit whisky. People going up or down the river, by night, may thus have seen flickering lights in the house or even silent figures moving to and fro. It doesn't take much to start such fictions."

"Probably," assented Tevvis, as he drew in toward his own pier at the lawn-foot.

He spoke with elaborate lack of interest, and even achieved a yawn. If this Indian was trying in joke to frighten him or to make him nervous, the joke was going to fall flat. As he moored the launch he turned to King and said:

"If you aren't in a hurry to get to Shuflin's, can't you come in for a little while? That will give you a chance to begin your longed-for exploration here. And it will give me a chance to offer you a smoke and something long and cool to drink. Come in, won't you?"

"I'll be more than glad to, if you aren't too busy," instantly answered King. "But if your painting will be interrupted ———"

Tevvis looked blankly at him before he remembered his own rôle of Garry Keith, artist. Then he assured King truthfully that he was not going to do any painting that morning. and he made mental note to have Gedge get out the easel and palette and colors they had brought down from New York to give credence to his artist character.

The two men walked side by side across the lawn and mounted the front steps. Then, at the same time, their gaze was fixed by a square of white paper pinned to one of the carved doors.

"My man must have gone downstream for provisions," suggested Tevvis, "and left a note telling me why he is away. But ——"

From the kitchen, out through the open windows, issued a raucously dreary sound that split the sweet silences of the wilderness morning. Gedge was singing at his work, and singing hideously. It was Gedge's one form of making known his rare moods of contentment. Now, sourly issued forth through the kitchen windows the whined ditty:

> "She say-y-ys, 'My deeer-est Hen-neer-ee,
> Should you upon me fraouwn
> You'd brek the heaart of Car-*o*-line
> Of Eeedinburrow Taouwn!'
> Sez 'eee ——"

"At least one of your men must be at home,"

ventured King. "Or is that a cat-fight we're listening to?"

Saul Tevvis did not answer. If Gedge was not absent, why was that square of white paper pinned to his front door? It had not been there when Saul went out, earlier in the morning.

King sensed the other's perplexity, and cut short his own laughing comment on Gedge's vocalizing. The two men went up to the door where hung the paper. It was a half-sheet of a scratch pad, torn roughly. Scrawled on it in pencil were the words:

> "*Get out. Get out* TODAY. *This is your third warning. It is your* LAST *warning. If you don't get out today you will get out feet frontward in a wooden box.*"

Tevvis and King read and reread the scrawl. For a moment neither of them spoke. Then King's breath was sucked through his white teeth in a sharp intake.

"The swine!" he snarled, hotly. "Mr. Keith,

I apologize to you, in the neighborhood's name, for such a silly trick. Some cracker boy stopped on his way up or down the river and did this to be funny."

"I think not," denied Tevvis. "The first warning was stuck into my drawing room, on the train, long before I got to Florida. The second warning was given to my servant, for me, by a negro. It isn't likely that a cracker jokesmith would have known what train I was coming on or in what drawing room on it. Then he couldn't have gotten here ahead of the train to give the second warning to Gedge. There appear to be several angles to this and several people concerned in it."

There was more annoyance than perturbation in his voice. King nodded approval of the Northerner's nerve. Then the Seminole asked, hesitatingly:

"The two other warnings? They were like this?"

"In effect. Both of them told me to keep away from here. I'm disobedient, by nature. So I came on. For the same reason, I shall stay. I am not a trespasser. I leased this place in good faith and for good money. If anyone wanted it, there were a hundred years and more for him or her to rent it or buy it. I'm going to stay and fight it out—if there's to be anything to fight."

"Good!" approved King, tersely. "You are a brave man, Mr. Keith."

"Why?" demanded Saul, nettled by the other's tone. "Where does the question of bravery come in? We're living in the twentieth century and this place isn't forty miles at most from Palm Beach. Nobody is going to risk punishment by killing or harming a stranger like myself, who is here only to mind his own business and do a winter's work. I tell you it's a joke. It's an elaborate joke, framed by some would-be humorist friends of mine. It can't be anything else. There'd be no sense in it."

"If you will pardon me for saying so, Mr. Keith," returned King, with worried gravity, "I think you are wrong. Of course I don't know what joke-playing friends you may have in the North, or whether or not they would be willing to spend so much money and so much time merely to give you a possible scare. But I can see a mush more plausible answer to the riddle."

"Go ahead," vouchsafed Saul, glumly, as King paused again, as if for leave to speak.

"I told you this tract of wild country is a refuge for bootleggers and moonshiners," said King. "It is also a hiding-place for other lawbreakers. In the heart of up-to-date Florida, this river section is still as primitive as it was in Colonial days. It attracts those who are 'hiding out' on one pretext or another, as well as those whose business won't bear the searchlight of the law. Its back reaches are impenetrable to anyone who doesn't know the secrets of its trails and inlets. You discovered that yesterday. Well, unless all reports I hear are wrong, there are secret activities hereabouts that are as hard to penetrate as the trails themselves. I think you have cut into one or more of those activities, in some way unknown to yourself, and that the persons concerned want to get you out of here—even, if necessary, 'feet frontward,' as this dirty anonymous warning says. That is all."

"I don't understand," protested Tevvis, impressed in spite of himself by the level-voiced and stolid-faced Seminole's evident uneasiness.

"It may be the bootleg ring," went on King. "Or it may be the moonshiners. Or it may be still another clique of lawbreakers to whom the use of this isolated house is desirable. Most probably the bootleggers. Their organized gangs have more money and more brains than any of the other lawbreakers around here. Isn't it possible they may have learned, through their men in Palm Beach, that you had rented this house, and then that they communicated with their agents in New York, who looked you up and had you shadowed, and then left that note for you in your train drawing room and telegraphed in code to the agents down here, saying when and how you were coming?"

"But ——"

"That would account for the first two warnings and the order in which you got them.

This third warning needs no explanation. Anyone could have sneaked out of the woods or up from the river and pinned it here. All he had to do was to make certain you were away from home. As, unquestionably, you're watched, that would be simple."

"I think you are entirely mistaken," contradicted Tevvis, none too civilly.

He could not tell this logician that the latter's very first premise was wrong, and that any bootleg agent in New York would have had an impossible task in locating and following a non-existent "Garry Keith." Nor could he tell King that the note on the train had been addressed to him not only by his own name but by his brand-new alias as well.

No, some one had found out his project for the winter, and his alias and the hour and the train whereby he was to start South; also that he was to meet Gedge at Jupiter. All of which was bewilderingly impossible, yet all of which must infallibly have happened. Puzzling as it was, it seemed to explode completely King's bootleg-spies theory, without giving any more plausible theory to go on.

"Our local law-abiding folk," resumed King, in no way offended by his host's curtness, "hold a complete neutrality with the local law-breakers. Through policy, we turn our heads the other way and purposely avoid seeing what we are not meant to see. In return, they do not molest us in any way and they don't thrust their lawlessness on our notice. But they may very readily resent the coming of an outsider —a government agent or a detective, for all they know—into the very heart of their working territory, to spy or to ask inconvenient questions or to tell later what he has seen or heard. I believe that is why they want you to clear out. Even if they could be made to see you are not a police official but only a harmless painter, they don't want you prying into their affairs or blundering accidentally upon something which may wreck them if it is babbled about. That is what I meant. Please don't be offended."

"I'm not," said Tevvis, ashamed of his own

grumpiness. "It's mighty kind of you to take so much interest, and I thank you. And it's good to have met you. I hope we shall see a lot of each other. Come in."

"Thanks," refused King, drawing back; "but on second thoughts, I think I'll get my business done downstream, and then stop here, if I have time, on my way home. If I can be of help to you, in any way at all—if this turns out not to be just a joke—please call on me for everything I can do."

He shook hands and then strode away toward the pier. There had been a ring of genuineness in his shy proffer of help. There had been true tact in his refusal to trouble further the perplexed Tevvis by choosing this time for an examination of Sea-Dream House.

Saul gave him admiring credit for both impulses. He liked the dark-faced lonely man. He looked forward with real anticipation to knowing him better.

Yet, Tevvis's innate "writer's sense" had kept hinting to him, from the moment of their meeting, that some intangible mystery hung about this solitary scion of the great Seminole-chief line, this man so high-bred and modern and well educated, yet dwelling by choice in a dreary hole like Boulding, when assuredly he must have wealth and culture enough to choose any pleasanter part of the civilized world for his home.

More and more this was borne in upon Saul. He loathed mysteries. Yet, for the past two days he had wallowed, perforce, in them. Back flew his mind to the most sharply annoying mystery of them all—Wanda Reeve's inexplicable change of manner toward him.

Resolutely, wrathfully, he thrust the girl from his thoughts. Into the house he stamped, and up to his circular stone study on the second floor. He resolved to get to work and to drown his mass of unprofitable conjectures in the concentrated zest of writing. More than once had he been able to find surcease from everything else, in this form of mental anæsthesia.

The study was lighted on three sides by round windows in keeping with the shape of the room itself. Except for the single chair and the typewriter desk and a waste basket, it was unfurnished. The desk had been turned toward the doorway, so that Tevvis need not face one of the three windows and thus be distracted by the view or by outside happenings.

Lifting his eyes from his desk, he need see only the uninspiring shut door in front of him, which had no phase of interest to draw his mind away from his writing. Like many of his craft, Saul Tevvis found this absence of external distractions needful to his utter absorption in the work he was doing.

Today, he put paper in his typing machine and prepared to carry on his synopsis from the point whither he had built it up so satisfactorily yesterday. But the task was not easy. To his dismay, he found his thoughts straying unbidden to Wanda Reeve and to fruitless speculations as to the reason for her strange shift of attitude toward him. With violent effort he thrust her abruptly from his mind.

But for only a few minutes at a time could he force his attention to center on the synopsis.

Ever his eyes and his fancy strayed from the typewriter keys. As there was nothing but blank monotony to observe on the door panels, he found himself studying absently the floor mosaics.

Savedra had imported or looted mosaic work for several of his rooms. The old ruffian, apparently, had been partial to this form of "stone embroidery" and had had rococo designs of it inserted in the walls and floors, with scant regard for artistic fitness.

For instance, in the dead center of this circular room was a circle of Florentine mosaic as big as a manhole; while at four edges of the stone flooring there were other and smaller patterns of it. Saul fell to tracing their intricate designs with his eye, as might an idle schoolboy who seeks to shirk the mastering of his lessons.

Frowningly he drove his mind back to his work, resolving to find a plain rug or carpet wherewith to cover as much as possible of the flaring floor-patterns and thus keep them from distracting him. As the plan came to him, he stopped typing once more, and scanned idly the central mosaic disk.

Then he winked fast, to clear his eyes of possible blur. For, while he was following the concentric swirls of the pattern, the disc seemed to turn, as on an axis. Slowly it revolved, for perhaps three-quarters of the way around. Then it stopped.

Tevvis rubbed his eyes. The room was flooded with noontide sun glare. This intense radiance, beating upon his unaccustomed retina, might well have caused the illusion.

Instantly thereafter Saul had every reason to believe this was true. For the mosaic disk began gradually to rise in air, as if pushed upward by cautious hands. It arose from its stone bedding for perhaps an inch, noiselessly, slowly.

With an exclamation, Tevvis leaped to his feet to investigate the impossible happening. In his scrambling haste, his heel caught against the chair leg, sending the heavy desk chair clattering to the floor and throwing Saul off balance.

He caught at the desk's corner to save himself from sprawling. Then, as he recovered his poise and strode forward to the tricky central mosaic, he focused his eyes once more on the disc.

It was firm-set in the flooring, as usual. There was no sign that it had risen an inch from its place. Saul rapped and kicked it, but it gave forth no hollow sound. He realized the sun glare had hoaxed his vision or else that the noonday heat had made him drowse for a moment and dream the mosaic circle was lifting itself out of the floor.

More than ever disgusted with his own newly-unreliable mental processes, he goaded himself back to work. But, stick to it doggedly as he would, he made but sorry progress. After two hours of forced activity, he picked up the sheets he had typed and read them. As he had feared, the day's work was wretchedly bad, unworthy of even an ambitious novice in literature.

Savagely he tore the sheaf of typed pages across, and flung them into the waste basket.

Then he opened his study door, that a cross-draught might ease the heat of the room.

On the threshold, pressed close against the door, Bunty had been lying. So, always, she lay against the outside of the door of whatever room her master might be writing in. For during Saul's work-hours Bunty was barred from his presence. She had a distracting way of scratching fleas, or of hunting for some imaginary prey under desk or chair, or of putting her head on Tevvis's knee to be patted, or of trying to lure him forth for a walk. None of these things was conducive to continuity of thought. Therefore, from puppyhood, the dog had been exiled while Saul was working.

Now she frisked into the room, greeting Tevvis as if their reunion followed a week's separation. She broke off in her gamboling about him, as she pattered across the center of the study. Nose to floor, she sniffed at the edges of the mosaic disc. But it did not hold her interest for more than a second or two, and then she was capering once more around her master.

"You're right, old girl," said Tevvis, aloud, "it's high time for a walk. I'm no use, for working, any more. Perhaps if we can get good and tired, on a ten-mile hike through the jungle and in the barrens, my alleged brain will clear and I can do an evening's work. It's certain I can't write anything but drivel, now. Come along. If that old idiot of a Gedge hadn't insisted on shutting you in the kitchen with him, for company, this morning, you'd have nailed the rotter who pinned that silly melodrama warning to the front door."

He pulled on a pair of hiking boots and picked up his stoutest walking stick. This time he had no intention of losing himself in the triangular tract of jungle-and-sand-hill maze, to eastward. He decided to stay within sight of the river, all the way out and back. That would enable him to hold his course. Later in the season there would be time enough to learn the back trails.

Along the bank he made his swinging way, in what developed presently into a breath-taking 'cross-country tramp. The going was painfully hard, except when he chanced upon a bit of sand-stretch or upon one of the natural glades where grew a plantation of wild cabbage palms. Here, except for logs and roots hidden by undergrowth, the walking was not bad. But elsewhere it was a struggle through liana and shrub and tangle, with no certain foothold.

Bunty enjoyed it hugely. She galloped hither and thither, squirming eel-like through thickets which Tevvis had to skirt, chasing an occasional squirrel or wood rat, stalking imaginary enemies in hollow trees. By rare good luck, the walkers came across no rattlesnakes though rattlers and cotton-mouth moccasins are the scourge of this bit of subtropic paradise. So Bunty's joy in the ramble was not marred by what, until last night, had been her one form of terror.

Sweating, breathing hard, comfortably tired by his hard exercise, Saul felt his puzzled brain swinging back to normal. With real anticipation he looked forward to the tackling of his novel. He whistled to Bunty and faced homeward.

In another quarter-hour he came again to the largest of the palm groves. Here he was able to walk with ease. Close to him on one side ran the river. A hundred yards or less to the other side the jungle wall bordered the landward end of the grove, in a natural rampart of vine and bush, pierced at intervals by some tall tree. Flaming air-plants pulsated like living coals from the upper boughs.

Along the river-bank side of the grove hurried Tevvis, his feet and Bunty's making a weird continuous rustling in the riffle of dry palm-fronds which carpeted the path.

Midway in Saul's passage of the clearing, two shots smashed the jungle silences. They were fired almost simultaneously, so close together that Tevvis could barely distinguish the lightning-brief interval between them. They came from somewhere behind that green rampart of jungle.

From behind that same wall of verdure, an instant after the two reports, issued a scream of torment. At the same time Saul Tevvis's Panama hat leaped from its wearer's head and fell to the frond-strewn ground several **feet** away.

A lock of Saul's hair left his head, along with the hat, and slid loosely down his face. The Panama had a neat round hole drilled through its band, toward the front.

By the time his hat had touched ground, Tevvis was in action. Swept by a gust of furious anger at the sneaking attempt to kill him from ambush, he charged at top speed toward the wall of green. Heedless of the fact that he was still an easy target for the unseen sharpshooter, he dashed across the clearing, as nearly as possible in the direction whence the nearer shot and the ensuing cry seemed to have come.

Over the treacherous footing he sped, pointing toward his goal and shouting to his collie:

"Get him, girl! TAKE him!"

There was no mistaking the fierce command in his voice. Bunty heard and read it aright. Instantly she hurled herself forward, like a flung spear, whizzing past her master and traveling with express-train speed. Her teeth were aglint from under her rage-wrinkled lips. Her hackles were abristle. Grimly she flew upon her punitive mission.

Far outstripped in the race, the panting and stumbling Tevvis continued the run at what pace he could achieve. Bunty crashed through the thick jungle screen and vanished. Then Saul could hear her snarl in wild-beast fashion as she leaped at her prey.

But before Tevvis could reach the green rampart her savage snarl merged into a whimper of fright. Out through the bushes into the clearing she raced, bobtail tucked between her legs, her ears flat, her whole lithe body athrob with fright.

From her foam-flecked jaws dangled something yellowish and ragged, that had been transfixed upon one of her curved eye-teeth and which still hung there unheeded by the panic-shaken collie.

Saul Tevvis did not stop, or waste thought on this astonishing cowardice of his stanch ally. He had but one purpose in his angry brain—he wanted to catch and punish the lurking assassin whose bullet had come so close to its human mark.

Into the jungle he threw himself, thrashing blindly through its myriad obstructions, ever pressing on toward the spot whence had issued the cry and the nearer shot.

On a leaf he saw a spattered drop or two of blood, then another on the branch of a bush. Following madly this hopeful clue, he penetrated another hundred feet or so into the tangle. There he came to the trunk of a high tree, with a yard or so of clear ground about its base. In an earth-hollow was a tiny pool of blood.

But, hunt as he would, he could find nothing more. At last, overheated and exhausted, he gave over his useless attempt to discover his assailant. The assassin doubtless was familiar with the jungle trails, as Saul was not. Moreover, the crashing of Tevvis's progress through the undergrowth would have been ample warning for him to elude his seeker.

Saul retraced his way toward the palm grove. As he came out into the open, a very shamefaced and humble Bunty trotted timidly forward to meet him. Tevvis frowned at her in bewilderment. She was the bravest and least nervous dog he had owned. Yet, twice within twenty-four hours she had fled in crazy terror, from—*what?*

She seemed pitifully aware of her own new cowardice and eager to be forgiven. But Saul had no eyes for her at the moment. During his absence she had clawed loose the yellowish object which her eyetooth had impaled during her first ferocious attack upon whomsoever she had discovered there in the jungle—during the moment of onslaught, before she had fled in craven terror.

The object was lying on the ground, near her. Tevvis picked it up and examined it. The thing was a hand-sized bit of cream-colored silk pongee, ragged at the edges and splashed with blood. The cloth was new and of excellent quality. But for the blood, it was clean.

Very evidently Bunty's shearing teeth had ripped it from its wearer as she sprang to the attack. Equally certain, her teeth had drawn blood. All this in the tiny space of time before mysterious fright turned her from a ravening avenger of her master's wrongs into a cowering poltroon.

"Bunty," mused Tevvis, half aloud, "that was a good bite. A deep bite. It explains at least some of the blood-spatters I found back yonder. It was no coward dog that leaped on a killer as you must have leaped on him. But what turned you into a coward, right afterward, old girl? That's the part of it that I wish I knew. I——"

He went silent. He was studying the pongee fragment anew. Twice, this day, had Saul seen silk pongee clothing of that color and of that same appearance of freshness. Such a suit had John King worn. Such a dress, too, had Wanda Reeve been wearing as she came up the garden path to greet him and as her smile of welcome froze into hostile contempt.

But he told himself that this detail of clothing was mere coincidence. In a radius of fifty miles, no doubt, there were hundreds of people, at this moment, clad in cream-colored silk pongee. So common was it in southern Florida in winter that an English visitor at Palm Beach, the year before, had asked if it were the uniform of the Floridian middle classes.

Besides, neither John King nor the girl would have fired on him from ambush. Tevvis was enough of a physiognomist to know that neither of them was of the "killer type," and that most assuredly neither would lie in wait for him in broad daylight and take a pot shot at him from behind a tree.

Chapter Seven

TEVVIS began to reconstruct the scene, back there in the woods, as best he might. There had been two shots, and then a shriek. Thus, evidently, only one of the two bullets had been meant for him. The other shot had been responsible for that yell of pain.

Some one had been in the act of firing at him, when some one else, at a distance, had seen the marksman and had shot him—presumably hoping to wound the assassin before the latter could pull trigger on his victim.

"Bunty," said Tevvis, petting the silken head raised so pathetically toward his hand in plea for pardon, "I seem to have had a friend, yonder in the jungle, as well as a foe. That's the only way I can figure it out. I wonder which of the two you tackled. Your teeth drew blood at the nearest place where I found traces of it. But that pool of blood, farther on, must have belonged to the man who yelped when my friend's bullet nicked him. You didn't get as far into the woods as that. But why didn't my rescuer come out and declare himself? Why did he and friend murderer *both* slink away?"

Sore perplexed, he retrieved his bullet-riddled hat and made his way back to Sea-Dream House. Gone was his hike-born steadiness of mind and gone was his renewed desire to settle down to work. His head buzzed with futile conjectures. His temper and his nerves were frayed past the point of a session of concentrated writing.

And this was the secludedly peaceful spot where he had been going to toil at his novel in such freedom from interruption and from outside disturbances as never before he had known! He grimaced with disgust at recollection of those happy anticipations, and at the ever-lessening hope of their fulfillment.

Nor, when he went to bed that night, would his overwrought senses let him dismiss the myriad puzzles that tormented him. To shift his thoughts, on the chance of falling asleep, he forced himself to review the wretchedly bad work he had been doing that day.

Yes, it had been worthless, that attempt to write consecutively and inspiredly. Or—had it? Perhaps his ruffled nerves had made him undervalue it. Perhaps he had been over-hasty in tearing it all up and flinging it into the waste basket. There might well be one or two bits of it worth keeping.

Early in the morning, Gedge would clean up the study, as usual. He would empty the waste basket and throw its contents into the kitchen fire. It might be well to salvage those torn pages, before then, and glance over them again in the hope of finding they were better than Saul had thought.

He got out of bed and groped his way toward the adjoining study. Instantly Bunty was awake. She jumped down from the foot of the bed and capered over to him in the dark, contriving to get between his knees, in her playful ardor, and all but upsetting him.

"Go back!" he commanded, crossly. "Go back to bed! *Up!*"

Obediently the little collie jumped back to her sleeping-place and cuddled down there. Tevvis found the study door and opened it. To make certain she should not follow him and trip him again, he closed the door behind him when he entered the pitch-dark circular room.

The stone flooring was chill under his bare feet as he felt his way along toward the desk and its waste basket. As he crossed the ice-cold paving, one of his advancing steps pressed upon nothing but air.

The floor was gone at that spot.

He shot down, feet foremost, through a narrow circular opening. Before he could catch hold of anything to break his fall he had landed with a jarring impact on a stone step many inches below.

Luckily, he landed on his feet, and his athletic training enabled him to recover his balance at once. There he stood in the dark, with the round edge of the flooring's aperture pressing against his knees, and with both arms outflung.

Back to his memory came that supposed optical delusion of the circular mosaic rising from its place in the middle of the study floor. He knew now it had been no delusion. The mosaic disc had been lifted clean from its socket in the stone. He could feel it lying alongside the hole it had covered—the hole he was standing in.

His bare toes explored their footing. He could feel the contour of a stone step. Reaching one of his feet downward, he felt another step below the first and at a different angle. This must be a curving interior stairway, leading up from the bowels of the house into the study, one of the clever architectural freaks that Savedra had fancied and had insisted on for his wilderness palace.

For the first time Saul was aware of loud barking from his bedroom and the imperative scratching of forefeet on the shut door. Bunty had heard him fall and had heard his exclamation of dismay. That had been enough and more than enough to bring the loyal little dog to the rescue of her supposedly endangered master. Her barks echoed clangorously through the still house.

Cautiously Tevvis climbed out of the hole and to solid flooring. Finding his way to the desk, he fumbled for matches and lighted his lamp. The illumination revealed the room precisely as he had seen it by day, except for the gaping round opening in its middle and for the mosaic disc lying beside it. A hinge held it to the casing.

He went to the bedroom and let Bunty out. The collie dashed into the study, making straight for the floor-hole and growling menacingly down it. Then she darted down the secret stairway, tense and raging. Assuredly there was nothing about her demeanor to suggest the cringing little coward of the afternoon.

Sharply Tevvis recalled her. With much reluctance she obeyed the summons, reappearing through the manhole and glaring backward down the black aperture. The study door flew wide. Saul wheeled to meet possible attack.

Gedge shambled in, holding a flashlight in one hand, while with the other he fastened the belt of the trousers he had pulled on over his curtailed nightshirt.

Waked by Bunty's clamor, the old fellow pushed his way into the study, as one eager for battle. Apparently he sought to wipe out the memory of the preceding night's terrified retreat. In a handful of words, Tevvis told him what had happened.

"Give me the flashlight," Saul continued. "I'm going down to investigate. This trap didn't open, all of itself. Bunty knows there's some one down there. I'm going to have him out, whoever he is. I'm getting tired of this haunted-house nonsense, and I'm going ghost-chasing."

"I'm in on it," declared Gedge, sturdily. "By your leave, sir, I'm going first."

"You'll stay where you are," ordered Saul. "The chap who opened this thing may still be upstairs somewhere. I don't care to have him come back while we're all down there, and fasten us in. You'll stay here. Hold Bunty.

You and she together ought to be able to give a fair account of yourselves, if he comes in here while I'm gone. Give me that flashlight."

Deaf to Gedge's objections, Tevvis took the light and began warily to descend the circling stairway. It ended in a vast low-ceiled room that seemed to be a sub-cellar. But Saul had no chance to find just what manner of place it was.

As he swept the darkness of the room with his flash, he heard a fierce intake of breath close behind him. Something knocked the electric torch from his hand, banging it to the earthen floor with a force that extinguished its light.

Before the light had fairly smitten the floor, Saul wheeled and grappled with the fast-receding figure which had knocked it from his grasp.

Seized by Tevvis's outflung hands as he was slipping out of reach, the unknown gave up his effort to get away and launched into a right ardent and tumultuous attempt to throttle his captor.

The two men reeled and stamped and

wrestled, there in the dense darkness, fighting silently and with maniac fury. But Saul Tevvis had had few successful opponents of his own weight, either on wrestling mat or in boxing ring. He was a trained athlete and he was still in the pink of condition. Moreover, he was spurred now by homicidal craving to overpower this midnight assailant of his and thereby perhaps find clue to the intangible and tormenting cloud of peril which had been settling close and closer about him for the past two days.

Even as Gedge, forgetful of orders, came shouting down the stairway behind him—even as Bunty wellnigh upset the Englishman by whipping past him down the stairs—Tevvis gained the hold he sought. A tightening, a twist, a heave, and his adversary lay wriggling and gasping on his back, with Saul's knee digging into his chest and Saul's ten fingers gripping his heaving throat.

"Go back and get a flashlight," Tevvis bade the descending Gedge. "Mine is broken. Hustle!"

In a few seconds the servant was back again in the cellar, carrying a new flashlight and his employer's service pistol. The torch's gleams were played upon the half-throttled and wholly subdued man whom Saul had pinned to the floor.

Tevvis's first view of his prisoner was disappointing. In the fight in the dark he had endowed the man with all kinds of mysterious attributes. But now he saw his opponent was merely a ragged and sallow "conch," lowest and most ignorant type of cracker, narrow of shoulder, dirty and stupid of face, an unworthy antagonist for any athlete.

"Take off that belt of yours," Saul commanded his servant, "and truss up his arms. . . . So. Now go ahead with the light. I'm going to run him up the stairs into my study. There we'll have a pleasant little chat with him. Let him alone, Bunty!" he finished, stemming the fierce efforts of the collie to hurl herself upon the captive.

Up the stairs, ahead of him and preceded by the light-bearing Gedge, Saul trundled the conch. Arrived in the lamplit study, his first move was to turn the prisoner over to Gedge and then to clamp shut the mosaic disk. Then he bound the conch's feet with a bathrobe cord and laid him helpless on the floor.

"Now," said Tevvis, cheerily, "you'll lie there and think, for a minute or two, while I get into some clothes. I'm going to dress, because when I'm through asking you a few hundred questions, I'm going to take you to Jupiter and turn you over to the police—unless you come through clean with the right answers. Think that over, too. I've heard you conchs are more afraid of the law than of anything else. Well, the law is what you're going to get, in a good ten-year dose, if you don't answer my questions or if you lie to me."

Purposely Tevvis gave his prisoner this few minutes for his nerves to wear raw before the inquisition should begin. He knew the dramatic value of suspense and he counted on it to crack the sullen obstinacy that glowed from the conch's pale eyes.

"Gedge," went on Tevvis, "you'll stand

there and keep on covering him with the pistol. If he stirs or if anyone of his lawbreaking little friends comes in, start the artillery going. Bunty," he added, pointing at the conch, "*watch* him!"

The collie stiffened to tense eagerness, crouching as for a spring, her gaze fixed avidly on the pinioned conch. Between the menacing pistol and the far more threatening dog, the captive was due to have a nerve-ripping three minutes.

Tevvis went into his bedroom, leaving the connecting door slightly ajar. There he proceeded to shed his pajamas and to dress. The process was not prolonged. In little time he was clad and shod.

As he dressed he rehearsed mentally the line of procedure his questions were to take. This ragged conch, very evidently, was not of the mental type to engineer such actions or motives as were becoming manifest toward Tevvis. At best, the fellow was a mere tool, the helper of some stronger spirit, the roustabout of some gang.

But he must certainly know who were his leaders and must know or guess something of the reasons which actuated their efforts to get Saul out of the way. He could be made to supply a clue which might unravel the whole annoying snarl of mystery.

By the time his boots were laced, Tevvis had figured out his proposed questioning. He went briskly into the study.

At his first step he noted something mildly peculiar. He remembered leaving the connecting door ajar. It was shut.

He opened it, visualizing the scene as he had left it a few minutes earlier—the bound and prostrate conch on the stone flagging; Gedge, grim and pistol-wielding; the fiercely-guarding collie; the wholesome flood of yellow lamplight illuminating the circular room.

As he opened the door, blackly impenetrable darkness smote upon Saul's eyes. The study was unlighted. Wide he swung the door, letting in a stream of radiance from his strong bedroom lamp. The rays made clear every detail of the study.

On the floor a man still was lying. But the man was Gedge. His pistol was gone and he was face downward on the flagging, moveless, his stumpy arms and legs spread-eagled awkwardly. The conch was gone. Where he had lain was a scatter of cut cords and belt leather.

Under the table cringed Bunty, her panting jaws foam-flecked, her shivering body pressed close to the stones, helpless terror vividly showing in every line of her.

The mosaic disc was back in place, as Tevvis had left it. There was no sign of foreign presence in the stricken room—nothing but the strew of severed bonds, the motionless sprawled body of Gedge, the quakingly panic-gripped collie.

Saul Tevvis stared agape. A sensation of something almost like horrified awe pringled through him.

Chapter Eight

HOT indignation shattered, presently, the amaze that gripped Tevvis. Once again the elusive powers of Sea-Dream House had bested him. More, they had outwitted him and made him ridiculous in his own eyes.

By rare good luck and by prowess he had overpowered and captured a tool of these powers and had left him under double guard. Now the conch was gone, Gedge was lying dead or senseless, and Bunty was in a state of blind terror. None of which made sense, but served to whip Tevvis's first blank awe into fighting anger.

Ignoring the collie as she crawled forth from under the desk to seek his protection, Tevvis bent over the prone Gedge, turning him on his back and searching for the source of his hurt. The manservant groaned dismally and opened his eyes, staring up dully at his employer.

Whatever might be the mystery of Bunty's fright, there was none as to Gedge's condition. A lump, half the size of a fist, was beginning to push up through the thin hair at the summit of his scalp, attesting to the sharp rap with club or gun-butt which had knocked him senseless.

"I'm—I'm a-watching him, sir!" mumbled Gedge, dazed and incoherent.

"I see you are," said Tevvis. "But just whom are you watching?"

Gedge's eyes rolled bewilderedly about the half-dark room. Then he heaved himself, groaning, to a sitting posture, his hands exploring his racked scalp while he peered from side to side in quest of his prisoner.

"What's—I say what's been and happened, sir?" he croaked, his voice thick with dizziness. "Just this second I was a-standing over him with the gun. And then, all at once it was—it was you what was a-standing over *me*. What's——"

"Somebody came in from the hallway, behind you, and knocked you over the head," explained Saul. "Knocked you clean out. Then he cut the conch loose and they both made a getaway. That clears it all up, except Bunty. She seems to have taken that propitious time to have one of her panic-fits. Must have had it before the man got to you, though, or she'd have given the alarm and gone for him. She ———"

Gedge lurched to his feet, heedless of the faintness and nausea from his hurt. His sour face went purple with wrath. Shakily he waved his clenched fists as he mouthed:

"Lemme at him! Lemme get my hands on the sneaking swine that crep' up on me from behind and slogged me. Lemme at him and I'll tear him into twelve pieces! I'll ———"

He sat down suddenly, overcome by a wave of dizziness. But instantly he struggled up again, pouring forth furious threats. The old fellow was mad clear through, craving revenge on the unknown who had made him false to his trust and who had felled him. The anger was helpful. For it cleared his head and set his blood and his heart to working again.

"I'll get him!" he vowed. "I'll get him if I have to stay at this God-forsaken place till I go to jail for smashing him. I'll get him, I'm a-telling you, sir! I ——"

"Yes," Tevvis soothed him. "I think I heard you the first time you said it. Meanwhile you'll get some witch hazel or some salve from the medicine chest and bathe that bump on your head. Then you'll go to bed again. You can't very well start out after him to-night. He'll be back in good time; he and the others of his jolly little coterie who are trying so hard to make our life pleasant here. Save your good breath and your better war-likeness till then. Go to bed. There'll be no more fun tonight. They're scared away and they know we're on guard."

"But, sir ——"

"Do as I say. Then, tomorrow morning you and I are going to make a search of that cellar place that the secret stairway leads down to. And afterward we're going to pile so many heavy weights onto this mosaic trap-door that all the ghosts and all the flesh-and-blood crooks on the Laxahatchee can't pry it up again. In that way, we'll stop *one* secret passage of this old blood-and-thunder pirate lair, anyhow. Go to bed. You'll need to be fresh for our cellar-exploring jaunt in the morning. We'll start in on it right after breakfast."

But next day, just as Saul Tevvis was finishing a belated breakfast and as Gedge was preparing the flashlights for their cellar expedition, a smart livery launch drew in at the pier.

From it debarked a large man who exuded prosperity from every inch of his immaculate white serge suit. He spoke to the launchman, then proceeded across the lawn toward the front door, eyeing the house with openly keen interest as he advanced.

"Gedge!" called Tevvis. "Another kind and loving neighbor is seeking to cheer our loneliness. Show him in here. Perhaps if he sees me at breakfast he'll take the hint and won't stay long."

Gedge departed on his mission; returning presently and ushering into the dining room the white-clad stranger. Saul arose with no enthusiasm and went forward to meet him.

At close quarters, Tevvis recognized the stranger with no difficulty at all. This man had been pointed out to him, not a month earlier, at a night club, and he had seen him again in a box at the Winter Garden.

He knew him for Norman Laigne, an industrious night-life *habitué* of Manhattan, a man of large means, and of a none-too-savory repute among the strait-laced. For the rest, Laigne was reputed to have engineered several none-too-upright business deals from time to time, and to have a mania-like hobby for collecting rare and costly antiques. His collections, along various lines, had been on view at more than one loan exhibition which Tevvis had chanced to visit.

But why such a Manhattan Island addict should be sojourning in the Florida hinterland or indeed anywhere else out of motor-ride from Broadway, Saul could not guess; nor what could be Laigne's business with himself.

"Mr. Garry Keith?" queried the visitor, with

suave cordiality, grasping Saul's unresponsive hand. "I am ——"

"You're Norman Laigne, aren't you?" interposed Tevvis. "I seem to remember hearing your name, last month, at the Flybynight Club. You were amusing yourself, as I recall, by pouring bootleg champagne down one of the saxophones, and the hostess threatened to have you thrown out."

If Saul expected to arouse any shame in his guest by this somewhat tactless reminiscence or by the faint tinge of contempt wherewith he mentioned it, he was doomed to disappointment. A truly beaming smile of fond recollection wreathed Norman Laigne's plump face.

"Yes, yes!" he laughed. "Quite! It was great fun. Yes, Tex Guinan said she'd have me thrown out. That's right, too. But of course she just said that to make a hit with the less frisky guests. No night-club hostess is going to throw out a man who spends six hundred dollars at her place every evening he goes there. Yes, I had paid my way for a bit of fun. And I had it. . . . I wish I could be as polite and say I remember seeing you there. But I was seeing things just a little on the bias that night. I remember some one told me this new writing wonder, Saul Tevvis, was there. I tried to get a look at him, but everything wabbled. Jack Barrymore was there, too. So was Arden Page."

Tevvis breathed a sigh of relief. So this talkative giant had not recognized him or penetrated his alias! That was well and more than well. Such a man could have been relied on, otherwise, to go back to Palm Beach and to prate loudly there about his call on the young celebrity. Then the lion-hunters would have descended on Sea-Dream House in droves. Yet, why was Laigne here?

The big man did not leave him long in doubt. In the next breath he came to the object of his visit.

"Mr. Keith," said he, in sudden seriousness, "I brought my wife down to Palm Beach, last week, because she has been very ill and because the doctors said that not only must she have the Florida winter climate, but also that she must have absolute seclusion, somewhere. Last year they made me take her to the Riviera, but this year they said Florida—Florida and quiet seclusion. So ——"

"So you brought her to Palm Beach?"

The irony escaped Laigne, who answered:

"Only till I could find the secluded and utterly out-of-the-way place hereabouts that the doctors said she must have for her rest cure. I asked the real estate agents. That is how I happened to hear of this house. And that is how I happened to hear you had just rented it."

Tevvis was giving only a half-ear to the smooth recital. Into his mind had flashed one of the several useless and untreasured bits of information he had heard concerning this antique-collecting rounder. When Saul had expressed disgust at Laigne's antics at the Fly-bynight Club, the man with him had said:

"Well, he's not accountable to anyone but himself, you know. He's been a widower for the past three months. Perhaps he's drowning his sorrow. Not that he ever paid any special attention to his wife while she was alive; but it's a good excuse for him to go back to the night clubs."

Hardly had Tevvis heeded the sneering comment. Yet now it came back to him with a rush. Laigne had just spoken of his wife— the wife he had taken to the Riviera last year, and whom he had brought to Florida this past week. Why should the widower go out of his way to tell such a needless lie to a stranger? Laigne hurried on:

"Yes, I was told you had rented Sea-Dream House and that otherwise it would have been the most ideal place in all Florida for me to bring her to. The quiet and the loneliness and the absence of anything that could excite her ———"

Tevvis recalled the happenings at Sea-Dream House during the past day or two, and he smiled at thought of the soothing influence they would have had on the nerves of an invalid—even on the nerves of this non-existent wife of Laigne's.

"When I set eyes on it this morning," proceeded the big man, "I saw they were right. It has everything she needs. I fell in love with the picturesque old place. That is why I have the courage to make a rather audacious request of you, Mr. Keith—that and the fact that I'd brave anything which might help my darling wife to get well. In short, I am here to ask you if you will consent to sublet to me."

"Huh?" asked Tevvis, perplexed.

"The agents told me the rent you have paid, cash down in advance, for your six-month lease here. I am prepared to take over that six-month lease, reimbursing you for the entire sum and adding a bonus of two thousand dollars. There is my proposition, Mr. Keith."

He leaned back, surveying Tevvis's lean face eagerly, seeking there the answer to his plea.

Saul had some ado to keep his expression immobile. Here was a Heaven-sent chance to get rid of an abode which he had learned to loathe—a house where he could not hope to do any satisfactory work and where mysterious intruders roamed by night. He could leave this jungle-region where unknown and unseen foes lay in wait to shoot at him during an afternoon walk, where his mind refused to grapple the problems of the novel he longed to write.

He could get out now without loss of self-respect and without running away from danger. Here was a good business offer. He would get back the lump sum he had paid for the house's occupancy, and he would pocket a two-thousand dollar bonus as well.

By a little patient search he could find a dozen places better fitted for his proposed winter of seclusion and work. His alias and his pose as an artist would serve quite as well elsewhere. Why stay longer in this impossible hole, now that he had a more than sufficient excuse to get out?

He tingled with mischievous joy at thought of the elaborate lie which Norman Laigne had devised in order to gain occupancy of Sea-Dream House, and of the pathetic touch about his devotion to the sick wife who did not exist. Laigne's eager voice broke in on him as Saul's lips were parted to assent to the proposition.

Worried by Tevvis's momentary silence,

Laigne mistook it and the coldly expressionless aspect of his host for haughty refusal to honor his proposal by so much as a curt "No." Wherefore he said, coaxingly:

"This means more to me than you realize, Mr. Keith. My wife is everything to me. Nothing else matters. For the bare chance of building up her shattered health there's nothing I wouldn't sacrifice. Two thousand dollars' bonus doesn't interest you? Very good. I'm no haggler. I'll make it an even ten thousand dollars, in addition to reimbursing you for what you've already paid out. There!"

Curiosity stirred deep down in Saul Tevvis's heart. Why should any sane man pay so egregious a sum for six months' rental of a house he might have bought outright for very little more money? It was absurd. What did Laigne want of the dreary old place? Why was he lying?

Laigne was not a bootlegger. He was not in hiding from the law. Queer as were some of his reputed business methods, he had been shrewd enough to keep on the right side of the civil and penal codes.

Then why should he want to bury himself in Sea-Dream House—he who was not happy out of sight of the Metropolitan Tower? Why should he pay a fortune for that doubtful privilege? Why should he, an expert business man, plunge from one offer into another five times as large, without so much as waiting until the first had been refused? Why should the sweat of worried eagerness be running down his suave face?

Then a twinge of conscience smote Tevvis. He would not have wished his worst enemy to blunder into possession of Sea-Dream House without first warning him of the possible dangers and the very certain mysteries encompassing it. On impulse he said:

"In the first place, you are said to be more than ordinarily well off, Mr. Laigne. Not that that is any of my business. But it means that you could take your invalid wife on a long and peaceful yachting cruise or you could buy or lease some large estate where she could have quite as much seclusion as she could have here. There are many such estates scattered through Florida. So I can't see why you should want to come here at all, or why you should be willing to pay so much for so little. Besides, it's only fair to warn you ———"

"I can afford to pay well for my whims," interrupted Laigne. "And I have taken a mighty fancy to this picturesque old ruin. Besides, I know that my wife will ———"

"That is what I was coming to," Saul took him up. "You say your wife is an invalid and must have absolute quiet and calm. Well, it's only fair to warn you she isn't likely to get either of those blessings here."

"You mean you won't ———?"

"I mean—and you can laugh at me for a fool if you like—I mean there are certain things about the place that I don't understand. I have proof there are people who want to get me out of here, and who have not hesitated at attempted murder in order to get rid of me. Also, there are people who have access to the house, through passages I don't know about, and who prowl here at night for some reason best known to themselves. Why, only last night ——"

He checked himself, gazing in astonishment at Norman Laigne. The big man was quivering from head to foot, as if in a hard chill. His plumply florid face went green-white. Its cheeks seemed sunken. Sweat poured from his forehead like rain. His eyes were abulge; his mouth fell slack. He was in very genuine terror—in the throes of some emotion that stripped him of his armor of self-control and left him pitiably craven with dread.

"So," continued Tevvis, taking pity on the man's wretched state by rising and crossing the room, and there standing with his back to Laigne and looking out over the river, that he might seem ignorant of his guest's humiliating condition—"so you see it is not a desirable winter home for a sick woman or for a man afflicted with nerves. And ——"

"Want to get rid of you?" babbled Laigne, wildly. "Prowl through the house at night, looking? The ——"

"I didn't say they were 'looking,'" Saul corrected him. "I don't know why they prowl through it when I'm supposed to be asleep. I don't pretend to know what their game is. But you see for yourself it is no place for you. If the bare mention of it scares you so, you'd better stay away and find some other quiet spot for the winter."

Tevvis spoke with increasing sharpness. He was annoyed at himself for the quixotic honesty which had made him point out Sea-Dream House's drawbacks and thus miss his own chance of getting out. He could not understand why so robust and daring a man of the world as Norman Laigne should have gone to pieces from fright on listening to the mere outline of the house's dangers. Well, the deal was off. Laigne would clear out, now, and leave him in peace. If ——

"Mr. Keith!" exclaimed Laigne, his voice still shaken by his strange excitement. "As I told you, we won't haggle. Here is my final offer: If you will give me legal leasehold here, this very day—if you will leave here today and leave me in possession—I will not only pay the six months' rent you agreed on, but I will give you my certified check for twenty-five thousand dollars. I mean it. I——"

"The man's stark insane!" Saul told himself. "He's crazy! That boatman out yonder is probably his keeper."

He glanced again at the pier where the launch skipper reclined on his back, smoking a cob pipe.

Around the sharp bend, from upstream, appeared a canoe. In the prow sat Mr. Reeve, clad in clerical garb, evidently on the way to hold service at one of the downriver settlements. In the stern, paddling the dingy-looking craft, was Wanda.

The morning sunlight shone like a shimmering benediction on her bright hair, touching her flower face with unearthly radiance. Very lovely and very young and very dainty did she look as her rounded arms propelled gracefully the rusty old craft. She turned her glance toward Sea-Dream House. For a mere instant her eyes and Saul's met, and held each other. Then, flushing hotly, she turned her head away.

Something gripped at Tevvis's heartstrings. A gush of strange tingling warmth swept through him, like the breath of God. Impulsively he wheeled to face the urgently appealing Laigne.

"You're wasting your time!" Saul cried, in queer exultation. "It isn't a question of money. Here I stay!"

Even as he spoke his eyes left the dumfounded face of the big man and strayed yearningly down the river in quest of the radiant girl whose passing had left the sunlit morning oddly dim and lifeless.

"I'm staying on here!" he continued, in that same thrill of exultation. "I'm not going away from—from—this. Please take my answer as final, Mr. Laigne."

But Norman Laigne did nothing of the kind. In alternate pleading and bonus-offering and at last in noisy rage, he pressed his point. Almost he went on his knees in crazed entreaty. Then his big voice boomed forth in foul denunciation of the stubborn fool who refused a fortune for the sake of staying on in such a place.

Saul listened in wordless astonishment to the uncontrolled tirade, wondering if Laigne were stark insane or only crazy drunk. Finally he cut in, his incisive voice piercing the louder and looser volume of sound:

"I think we've both had about enough of this," he said, sternly. "If you are out of your mind, I am sorry. But there is no reason why I should be made deaf because of it. You have had my final answer. There is nothing to detain you here any longer." He went to the door and opened it. Laigne stood still for a long half-minute in the middle of the room, his face gradually resuming its mask of florid suavity.

"I've given you your chance," he said, presently, his tone muffled and dead. "Yes, you've had your chance. I'll go now."

He brushed past his host and out into the sun's glare. Tevvis watched him board the launch, and then watched the launch disappear down the river.

"He's not crazy," Saul murmured to himself, "and he's not drunk. When he went away he was as sane as I am. What made him so wild to get this house, that he threw away his self-control and wanted to throw away his money with it? What do the rest of them want here? *What's in this house, anyhow?*"

Gedge appeared in the doorway, from the kitchen. He was carrying two flashlights. In his belt was stuck a long carving-knife. The old fellow was little the worse for the crack on his thick skull. Bunty pattered at his heels.

"Funny gentleman, that," said Gedge, nodding in the general direction whence Norman Laigne had disappeared. "When he got so noisy-like, it was all I could do to keep Bunty from barging in. She appeared to think he was going to hurt you. I couldn't help a-hearing some of what he said, even when I only listened halfway hard. Wasn't he offering you a mort

of money to let him come and live here, sir?
—if it's any of my business."

"It isn't," answered Saul, "and he was.
What do you suppose he wanted it for?"

"For the pirate gold, of course," said Gedge,
with no hesitation at all. "That's what they're
all after. The folks and the ghosts and all."

"What pirate gold?" demanded Tevvis.
"What are you talking about?"

"Why, the pirate gold that Mr. Savedra
buried here, of course!" explained Gedge. "He
was a pirate. And it comes as natural for a
pirate to bury his treasure as for Bunty here
to bury a bone. It's pirate nature. That's
what it is, sir. Everybody knows that. They're
born with it."

"Every dime-novel sea-story reader knows
that," returned Saul, amused by the man's
simple faith in the hoary fiction of interred
wealth. "But everyone with brains knows it's
absurd. Use your own common sense and
figure it out. In the first place, every mer-
chant ship in old days wasn't laden with treasure. Mighty few of them carried any quantity

of it.   And treasure ships had too strong an escort of men-o'-war to make them safe prey for pirates.   The average pirate picked up less wealth than the average shopkeeper does.   And he never buried it unless he happened to be on a cruise and wanted to get more without endangering what he had.   Even then he'd naturally go back and dig it up as soon as the cruise was over.   It was only when he happened to be sunk, during the cruise, that the treasure stayed buried.   And not then, if any of his men could escape and go back for it.   As for Savedra, he had no reason to bury his wealth here.   Why should he?   It's on record that he had big accounts in a dozen banks in the West Indies and in Europe.   Why should he bury treasure here, for any member of his crew or of his household to steal?   Just forget that buried-treasure fake, Gedge."

"Yessir," assented Gedge.   "And it's his buried treasure they're after, like I said.   Maybe you and me can find it sometime while we're here."

Chapter Nine

WITH a groan, Tevvis gave up the hope of hammering sanity into his servant's brain. With Gedge, a fixed idea was a fixed idea. Words never shook it.

"The pistol being gone," went on the servant, "I made bold to sharpen up this carver, in case we was to run across that cuss who slogged me over the head, while we're exploring down-cellar. You said for me to make ready as soon as breakfast was over. The dishes can wait. Shall we start now, sir?"

Laigne's visit had driven from Tevvis's mind the project of investigating the cellar, but, at the reminder, he was on his feet.

"Get something to draw out these nails," he bade Gedge as they came to the massive door leading from the kitchen to the lower regions, "and an ax to smash these rusty old locks. The nails somehow don't look so rusty or so ancient as the padlocks. We'll start from here, instead of going all the way upstairs and down through that corkscrew secret stair. No use taking a secret way when a public way is shorter and easier."

With some difficulty the padlocks were struck off and the long and cumbrous nails drawn. On stiff hinges the door was pushed open. Adventurously, Tevvis and Gedge, preceded by the highly interested Bunty, descended the wide steps to a wholly empty and dim-lit cellar which extended for perhaps half the area of the house. High and small and barred and dirt-grimed windows admitted a trickle of dull light.

Tevvis made a round of the empty space, playing his flashlight on the gray-raftered ceiling rather than on the walls. Then he announced:

"This isn't the cellar I was in last night. See, there is no corkscrew stairway leading down into it. This is the house's regular cellar. The other is a secret one. This cellar hasn't been used, even for storage, in centuries.

Come up to my study and help me pry open that disk in the floor."

Two minutes later the men and Bunty were climbing down the corkscrew stairs from the study. They emerged into a cellarway, about the same size as the first but wholly different in aspect. Here were no windows. But here were bins and vaults and a clutter of strewn rubbish. On the dust of the floor were round dents where casks had stood. The bins and alcoves were set deep into the walls. But they were empty.

"Not so terrible exciting," commented Gedge when they had made a careful round of the cellar and had rapped the walls in vain for a hollow sound. "By your leave, sir, I think I'll go back to washing the breakfast dishes. I was hoping maybe we'd find why those folks use it and how they get out after they come down these funny stairs. But it's no go. Ghosts has got ways we don't understand, I s'pose."

He clumped laboriously up the circular steps, leaving Saul to continue his vain investigations with Bunty's fussy assistance. For a minute Tevvis stood there, his light playing fitfully on the dust-choked walls and floor. He was pondering part of Gedge's grumbled farewell—"How they get out after they come down these funny stairs."

Naturally, the intruders did not descend the corkscrew stairs for the fun of going back again, nor had Savedra's crafty architect designed merely a blind passage. There must be egress. Saul's eye fell on a scrap of dirty rag among the rubbish. It was khaki-colored. He had seen its like on the conch he found here. He remembered, too, in the course of the short wrestle, a handful of his opponent's shirt had come away in his grasp.

Tevvis picked up the soiled wisp of rag and called Bunty over to him. Holding the cloth to her sensitive nostrils, he commanded:

"Find him, Bunty! Go *find* him!"

It was an old game between master and dog, this giving Bunty something to sniff at and then bidding her find its owner. Gayly as ever, she entered into it. She sniffed daintily and then deeply of the dirty shirting. Then she circled the cellar at a hand-gallop, nose to earth, afterward quartering the floor as a bird dog quarters a stubble field. ,

Suddenly she darted off at a tangent, whimpering softly and eagerly. Her new course brought her to the foot of a dusty and empty bin. Here her nose ran along the base of the bin from side to side. With a worried bark, she turned and faced her master, immediately afterward nosing the bottom of the bin again.

"Yes, old girl," said Tevvis, in disappointment. "I don't doubt he sat there or stood there. That was the direction he came from when he hit the light out of my hand. But how did he get in here?"

Again the collie whimpered, and again she glued her nostrils to the base of the bin. Tevvis strolled across, playing his light on the high wooden receptacle. Then he flashed the light into its interior. The bin was empty.

But against one of its sides—a spot whence the dust and soot had somehow been rubbed away—he saw a darkly greasy patch as though many hands had been pressed there. It was at a juncture of two back-boards, one of which jutted beyond the other. There seemed no reason why that one place should be shiny with much pressing and that the surface dust should not be there as elsewhere.

Idly Tevvis leaned over the bin-side to investigate. He touched the shiny spot, perhaps six inches in diameter and rough in contour. Nothing happened. But in leaning over he almost lost his balance. To right himself he thrust hard against the greasy surface.

Immediately, and as if on oiled hinges, the bin swung sidewise, outward against the cellar wall. There was no squeaking and there was no friction.

A black opening was revealed. Under the flash of Saul's light, this resolved itself into a vaulted and low passageway leading out under the ground. Its earthen floor was trodden hard and smooth as though by hundreds of bare feet.

Here was a tunnel, neatly drilled or hewn through the coralline hardpan which everywhere underlay the surface loam. In one or two places the roughly curved roof was shored up by ancient timbering. But for the most part the ceiling was of smoke-smudged white coral rock.

Atingle with boyish anticipation, Tevvis held his electric torch in front of him and entered the tunnel. Bunty ran joyously ahead, on her errand of tracing down the owner of the shirting. Saul whistled her to heel, and led the way. The roof was at least eight feet high. The passageway was fully four feet wide.

Some five yards beyond the cellar the tunnel split into a "Y." The left fork led at a sharp angle from the right, for perhaps another five yards. Then it ended in a flight of stone steps that went upward. The right fork continued on, at a gentle downward slope, out of Saul's range of vision.

Tevvis turned into the left split of the passage. Reaching the low stone steps, he climbed them. Their smooth treads proved them to have been oft-used. They ran up to a blackened circular wooden slab, with a hinge at one side of it. This hinge was little rusted. Its grooves shone as with recent oiling.

Saul pushed it upward. Because of clever balance and of new oiling, the slab yielded readily to his push. It lifted, and he climbed into an octagonal little room of carved marble. The room's door was padlocked from within, and the lock was neither antique nor rust-covered. Through marble fretwork, fingers of white sunlight filtered, making needless the beams of the electric torch.

Saul peered out through one of the frets of openwork. He found himself looking directly at the porch of Sea-Dream House.

Now he knew well where he was. He was standing in the little rococo stained white-marble summer-house on the lawn at one side of the house's front door. More than once since his arrival he had looked in at the interior of the summer-house, through these loopholes of marble. As it was unfurnished and seemed of no particular interest, he had not tried to force its locked door.

Savedra, very evidently, had devised a clever way of escape from the house, in event of attack by savages or freebooters or by the law. These cunningly wrought loopholes, too, afforded murderous opportunity to fire, from the safety of the summer-house, upon any hostile body of men who might be assailing the house from the front porch.

Remembering the other fork of the tunnel, Saul whistled to Bunty and set forth to explore it. It led for perhaps two hundred feet, still slightly downward and to the left; ending at a locked door. This door's padlock was ancient and rust-eaten. The door's hinges were coated with rust, undisturbed. Old cobwebs were spun across and across the portal. No sign of recent use here; even as this fork of the tunnel was far less smooth-beaten of footway than had been the left fork.

With a kick, Tevvis smashed the rusted padlock. Scraping some of the rust from the hinges with his pocket-knife, he flung his hundred and sixty pounds of muscular weight against the door. Soggily, groaningly, it collapsed under his shove. On protesting hinges it sagged outward.

Saul stepped warily forth, into a sun-shot pocket of dark green which gave forth a spicy smell. Once more he knew where he was. He was in the heart of a clump of boxwood. There was only one such clump on the grounds —a giant patch of fragrant box which stood a few yards from the water's edge, on the margin of a whitish sand-patch, a hundred feet or so upstream from the dock.

The box had been trimmed, long ago, into the shape of twin Spanish galleons. But centuries of neglect had all but obliterated the resemblance. It grew at the extreme upper end of the grounds.

Tevvis had wondered more than once why the pier had not been built at the edge of this single bit of natural sandy beach instead of in its present inconvenient location. He had been planning to go swimming from this sandspit, some day.

He parted the box boughs to step out upon the smooth expanse of sand—perhaps twelve feet wide and with some twenty-seven feet of it between him and the water. Bunty, as usual, pushed on ahead of him.

But at her first onward step the little collie wheeled and flung herself bodily upon her master, crowding him back into the clump with all her wiry strength. She was growling in angry warning. When her weight could not avail to check his advance, she caught Saul fiercely by the trousers-leg and braced herself, dragging backward.

Annoyed by her persistence and deeming this another manifestation of her recent queer spells, Tevvis thrust the dog roughly to one side and stepped out upon the sand.

At his first stride the man sank ankle deep.

Now it was plain why the dock had not been built here and why this corner of the grounds was neglected. The whitish stretch was a Florida quicksand, treacherous, deadly, smoothly deceptive of appearance.

Back shrank Tevvis. But he was caught. As fast as he dragged forth one foot from the sticky mess, the other sank deeper. Presently, he was almost up to his knees in it.

Gallantly Bunty flashed forward on the first instant, her dainty white paws sinking deep at every floundering motion. She had sought desperately to warn her master back from this trap against which her own instinct had warned her. Failing, she was disregarding her own terror at the danger and was trying tenfold more desperately to drag Saul back to safety.

She tugged frantically at Tevvis's coat hem, seeking to brace her feet that only sank the lower as the quicksand sucked at her and at Saul. She could gain no good leverage, and at best she weighed less than fifty pounds, as against Tevvis's hundred and sixty.

She made no progress and she was in ever greater peril of being engulfed. Yet gayly and gallantly she kept on at her hopeless task; the little dog that had shrunk beneath the desk in mortal terror a few hours earlier.

Fiercely, Saul commanded her to go back to the safety of the boxwood clump. For once in her obedient life, she gave no heed to his orders, but continued to tug flounderingly at the luckless man's coat in her pathetically futile attempt to extricate him.

Marking time, to delay the suction's pull upon his own half-buried legs, Tevvis stooped and picked her up by the nape of the neck, yanking her free of the sand, and flinging her bodily into the river, twenty feet in front of him. The exertion made him sink perilously deeper.

"Back!" he yelled to her, as she made as though to return to him. "Find Gedge! FIND him!"

Once more the little collie disregarded her deity's orders. True, she did not return to the quicksand, but neither did she go in quest of Gedge. Instead, she struck out downstream barking loudly and swimming at full speed, with head and shoulders high above water.

She had seen something which now caught her imperilled master's eye.

From below, a canoe was gliding into the space before Sea-Dream House. Its only occupant was Wanda Reeve. Evidently she had taken her father to his destination and was paddling homeward again to Boulding. The barking and splashing collie attracted her notice. Thence her glance fell upon the struggling Tevvis. Instantly the canoe shot forward at racing speed. As she propelled it Wanda called imperatively to the man:

"Stiffen your whole body! Keep it ramrod stiff! Now throw yourself forward on your face, with your arms stretched out. *So!*"

Instinctively Saul followed the silver-voiced commands. He stiffened and then flung his rigid body forward. As he was little more than knee-deep in the crawling quicksand and as the chief weight of his body was well above the surface, the maneuver served to drag his feet and calves out of the sticky trap, though with a wrench that threatened to snap the bones.

Forward he wriggled, spread-eagle, toward the canoe. Twice, from the prow, Wanda tossed the slenderly strong tie-rope before his clutching hand closed over it. Then, bracing the paddle against the firmer bottom of the

river shallows, she made him drag himself onward, hand over hand, along the rope.

By inches, at first, then faster, Tevvis pulled
himself along the treacherous surface, while
Wanda strained every young sinew to maintain
her leverage on the braced paddle. Bunty
swam around and around the boat, still barking reverberatingly.

A last heave and there was clean and non-
clinging water under Saul, instead of the claw-
ing sand. Another stroke and he was alongside the panting girl.

"Thanks!" he gasped, momentarily spent
with his mighty exertions.

"Don't try to talk," she bade him. "Get
back your breath and your strength first. Hold
lightly to the gunwale, if you can. I'll tow
you to the pier."

Now that the peril was past, her manner
had relapsed to the frigid hostility of the preceding day. Through his own fatigue and reaction, Tevvis noted this change, with a pang.
The canoe reached the pier in a few long sweeps
of the paddle. Tevvis climbed up on the low-

est step of the dock, Bunty clambering alongside him.

The collie was hysterical with rapture over
her master's escape. Shaking a cascade of river
water from her heavy yellow coat all over him
and over Wanda's light dress, Bunty galloped
in drunken circles around the lawn-foot, checking her race at every few seconds to leap on
Tevvis, trying to lick his face.

Wanda started to push off upstream, without
speaking again, as soon as the man was safely
on the pier step. But Tevvis would not have
it so. He reached out and laid a detaining
hand on the canoe's gunwale. In haughty astonishment at the action, she stared icily at
him.

"Wait!" he said. He blurted out his words
impulsively. "You aren't going away like this.
You—you saved me from a rather vicious
death. I don't know the right words to ——"

"Then please don't trouble to say them," she
cut him short. "I am afraid I am not interested. Will you kindly let go of my canoe?
I ——"

"No," he refused, in sudden indignation, "I won't! Not till you've told me what I've been unlucky enough to say or do, to make you change from the friendly way you treated me when I met you first, and why you treat me as if I was something—something slimy!"

"Aren't you?" she asked, her level brown eyes contemptuous. "Aren't you 'something slimy,' Mr. Saul Tevvis, alias Mr. Garry Keith? If not, I can't think of a better definition for you. Now will you kindly let go of the canoe and ——"

"No," he cried again. "I won't! I've done nothing to make you look at me and speak to me like that, Miss Reeve. And you're going to do me the justice to tell me what you mean. You are, if the rest of you is as honest as your eyes. You helped me out, the other evening, when I was lost in the woods back yonder. You asked me to lunch with you and your father. When I saw you, next morning, you withdrew your invitation and you all but ordered me out of your house. I had done nothing, overnight, to warrant that. I ——"

"Perhaps not," said Wanda, "but when I met you in the dusk I didn't know you, except as Garry Keith, a Northern painter who had come down here to do some sketching. When I got a clear view of you, next morning, I recognized you. I have seen your photograph, of course, in the papers. And I heard you speak, two weeks ago, at the Authors' League dinner, when I was visiting my aunt in New York. I had a good view of you then, and I recognized you, past all doubt, the instant I saw you by daylight. So ——"

"I don't deny I'm Saul Tevvis," declared the man. "But I do deny that I've ever done anything to make a good woman, young or old, refuse my acquaintance and order me from her home. I ——"

"No?" she queried, while Saul realized miserably that he was not at his outward best, crouching there in soaked and sand-smeared clothes and with a rivulet of muddy water trickling from his forelock down his nose. "No? Perhaps not. I am afraid our ideas of ethics differ very widely, Mr. Keith Tevvis. To

skulk down here under a false name, for the
sake of writing some unpleasant muckrake book
about the neighborhood that will not only bring
down the law on a throng of half-starved crackers, but will make our quiet region notorious
and open it to the police and to a swarm of
Yankee tourists, and ruin its sweet primitive
life—to destroy the one unexploited corner of
ancient Florida—to harm people who never
harmed you and who are prepared to offer you
hospitality—in short, to play the snake in the
grass—well, that may not seem 'slimy' to you.
But less sophisticated folk, like myself, don't
care to associate with a man who does such
things. And ——"

"Neither would I," agreed Saul. "In fact,
I'd refuse to associate with such a man, my-
self. But I don't happen to be that man, Miss
Reeve. May I ask who told you I am?"

"I didn't need anyone to tell me," she re-
torted. "In your speech at the Authors' League
dinner you said New York was no place to
work in and that you would have to leave town
before you could begin the new novel you were

going to write as soon as possible. You left town. I read in the paper that you had sailed for Abyssinia in search of local color for your new book. Then I found that was just a blind and that you had come down here, instead, for your local color. Such a book, written by a novelist as popular as you are just now, will wreck this home region of mine that I love. Do you wonder ——"

"I have no way of making you believe what I'm going to say," again interrupted Saul, "except that you will know, when the book is out. It is true I came down here to write my next novel. I came here under another name and I pretended I was going to Abyssinia. If I didn't do something like that, to get away from people, I knew there was no faintest chance for privacy or for the concentrated work the book calls for. That's why I ran away from everyone. Not that it's done me any great good, thus far. But there was nothing dishonorable—nothing 'slimy'—about it. I demanded the same right to privacy that is given to a bookkeeper when he is doing night work or to a tenement dweller in his own home. I demanded the right to be by myself and to do my work in peace. The only way I could hope to do it was ———"

"By coming here and spying for rudimentary local customs and for the lawless life of ———"

"As I told you," he went on, unheeding, "I can't prove to you—I can't do anything except give you my unsupported word, as a man and a Mason—that my book is not going to have any Florida scenes or Florida secrets in it. It won't even mention the state of Florida, to say nothing of this hidden neighborhood. Its general plan was all worked out in my head months ago, long before I even thought of coming here. I happened to pass Sea-Dream House, on a fishing trip, a year or so back. I remembered it and it seemed out-of-the-way enough for my purpose. So I leased it.

"When my book is published, and if you do it the honor of glancing it over, you will see I have told you the truth. Its scenes are all laid in the mid-Western town where I was born. Till then I have no way of making you believe me. . . . Lord! but it's hard to be convincing and eloquent with four gallons of river water slopping down between my shoulders! And when I must be looking like Charlie Chaplin at his Chaplinest!" he broke off, with a rueful laugh.

Chapter Ten

FOR a moment her dainty face strove to maintain its judicial aloofness. Then, in spite of herself, she joined in his laughter. If there was a tinge of hysterical relief in her laugh, it was none the less musical, and it went to the very heart of the bedraggled man. Together, for no logical reason at all, they laughed. The sound of their dual mirth rang out gayly on the river silences, and it did more than ten thousand mere words to wipe out the memory of the past day.

Tevvis checked himself, and asked in sudden boyish eagerness:

"You believe me, don't you? *Please* do. It's the truth. And I've been so miserable ever since yesterday morning!"

There was a softness in her laughing eyes as she made impetuous answer:

"You know perfectly well I believe you!

And, oh, I'm so ashamed I was horrid! It was more on my own account than on yours. You see, I loved your book. It was wonderful. And when I saw you, in New York, you looked just the way I had hoped you would. So many authors don't, you know. They're so— so *shaggy*. Or else ratty. And when I met you in the dusk—of course I didn't know you for the man whose book I loved—it seemed splendid to have such a neighbor in this desolate place, and I was ever so glad. Then, next day, when I saw you—a billion air-castles all came crashing down and I was furious. More at myself than you. And ——"

Their hands—his wet and dripping, hers cool and little—somehow had clasped. Now, in belated self-consciousness, she drew hers away.

"You didn't happen to see me, at that Authors' League dinner, did you?" she asked, changing the subject and talking very fast. "I was sure you couldn't. Because there were so many people there and you never happened to look in my direction. But yesterday, at the first instant you looked at me, it seemed almost as if you suddenly recognized me. You couldn't, of course, but ——"

"But I did," he made answer. "I saw you twice, on the train coming down here from New York. Neither time did you look at me. But I was rude enough to stare at you as if I'd never seen another woman. Then, when I saw you yesterday —— By the way, did you happen to have any friend or escort on board who knew me? Because a note was left in my drawing room—with both my own name and my alias on it."

"No, I came down all alone. Dad met me at Palm Beach, and my aunt put me on the train at New York. But I traveled alone. Why did you think a friend of mine sent you a note? Was it written by anyone around here?"

"Probably. Almost certainly. It was anonymous."

Her smiling eyes clouded. Into her manner came the faintest hint of her former stiffness.

"An anonymous letter?" she asked. "And

you say it 'almost certainly' was written by some one around here. I'm sorry you have such wretched opinion of your new neighbors. We ——"

"At least I have a very definite opinion about them," he answered, with forced lightness. "One of them put a bullet through my hat yesterday. Another had an industriously melodramatic fight with me in the cellar back there. Another knocked my man servant senseless and stole my pistol. Three of them have sent me unsigned warnings to get out of here if I value my life. Apart from that, they seem to be an uncommonly fine body of men. They certainly do their best to keep my days and nights from becoming dull."

Her face was tense with troubled unhappiness.

"Will you please tell me what you mean?" she asked, in childlike worry. "I don't understand. Honestly I don't."

Concisely, yet omitting no detail, he told her the story, beginning with the note he had found under the magazine in the train and concluding with Norman Laigne's strange conversation of an hour agone.

By way of proof, he drew out from his inner coat pocket a sopping square of crumpled paper he had thrust there. It was the third warning, the one Saul and King had found pinned to the front door. Wanda scanned the scrawled words, her brows knitting.

"It is terrible!" she exclaimed, shuddering.

"Not so very," he argued. "I've seen worse handwriting. Of course the paper is pretty wet, just now. But ——"

"Oh, I don't mean that!" she denied, a catch in her voice. "You know I don't. I mean the whole thing is *horrible!* It's unbelievable, too. But ——"

"Many things are unbelievable, Miss Reeve. But a lot of them happen, just the same. I wonder if you can clear up any of the tangle for me? You say you've always lived down here. So you must have heard all the rumors about Sea-Dream House and you must have heard of the various classes of people here who don't scruple to shoot men's hats off or to wander by night through this house I've rented. Can you give me any kind of clue? Or would you rather not? I'm wondering chiefly why people are sneaking around the secret stairs of Sea-Dream House. If they're looking for something, they've surely had a century or more to explore it from top to bottom, when it was empty. What made them wait till *I* got here, and what are they after?"

"I can only tell you such scraps of news as Dad has happened to pick up from the crackers and passed on to me. The crackers love him. But they know how he disapproves of many of the things they do. So they are reticent in talking to him about anything he may not approve of."

"I see. But ——"

"Whatever I know or whatever I've heard, I'll tell you gladly," she went on. "And I'll do more. Dad has tremendous influence among the crackers. He has devoted his whole life to them and to the Seminoles. I'll tell him the things you've told me, if I may. And he will go to them and make them leave you alone. If you're known to be Dad's friend, it will be a wonderful protection to you. Honestly it will. They adore him."

"Thank you. It's mighty kind of ———"

"As to the things I've heard: It is pretty well known that this reach of the Laxahatchee is used for the running and hiding of illicit liquor cargoes, and it is pretty well known that the cellars of Sea-Dream House have been used, more than once, to store such cargoes in, when it wasn't safe to carry them inland or when a revenue raid was coming. Nobody, as a rule, dares venture in there. So it is a safe hiding-place."

"The bootleggers or the conchs probably know of the secret passages and all that hocus-pocus," supplemented Tevvis, "and they know about the hidden cellar. No revenue men could ever find that. But they may be afraid I shall blunder onto it. It may have been a bootleg crew transporting booze from the cellar to one of their river craft that I thought I saw from my window, the first night, and that Gedge heard the night before."

"Perhaps," she assented. "Perhaps they were moving it to some safer place. But they were taking tremendous chances of your catching them at it."

"It would have been somewhat like my catching a man-eating tiger, I fancy," he said. "The 'catching' would have been the other way around. But they could easily have gotten in and out of the cellar, with the stuff, through the summer-house. That would have been the simplest way. Heavy loads of liquor couldn't well have been carried up and down the secret corkscrew stairway. In fact, there'd have been no sense in doing it. So why should bootleggers climb up that way to the second floor, at night? And what was the man doing up there who crept behind Gedge and stunned him?"

"I don't believe he was a bootlegger or had anything to do with the liquor gang," answered Wanda. "I believe he was one of the treasure-hunters."

"The—*what?*" asked Tevvis, marveling at her matter-of-fact mention of the word.

"The treasure-hunters," she repeated. "There

has always been a firm belief that Saveu.
hid a fortune in jewels and in gold, somewhere
about the house or the grounds here, and that
he left a chart showing just where he had hidden the treasure. In fact, a cracker family has
a tradition that a grandfather of theirs once
rummaged through Sea-Dream House looking
for something worth stealing and that he ran
across the chart. He didn't know what it was,
but he told his son about it. The son didn't
know, either. But after his father was dead
he happened to describe it to some one with
more brains, and he said it was a treasure chart.
But the son didn't know whereabouts in the
house his father had found it."

"The same dear old treasure-chart yarn!"
laughed Tevvis. "I was hoping this mystery
was going to be more original than to make
use of such a dreary prop. The buried-treasure rumor is ridiculous enough, without adding
the chart fake to it."

"True or not," she insisted, "loads of people
believe it. Perhaps, when they heard you were
coming here, they thought you had rented the

house so you could look for the treasure in peace. That may have fanned the old rumors and set people on a new frantic hunt for the missing chart. Don't you think that's possible?"

"Anything's possible. The more impossible it seems, the possibler it's likely to be. Still, that doesn't account for Norman Laigne. He is no maniac treasure-hunter. Even if he had heard there was a story of gold and jewels hidden here, he'd know there couldn't be more than a very few thousand dollars' worth of it, at most. Nothing worth his wasting six months of time in seeking. No, something bigger than either bootleg cargoes or fairy-tale pirate treasure brought Laigne here. He's a financier and a professional collector. But when I told him there were mysterious people already sneaking about the house, he was half-delirious with fright. He must have been afraid they'd get ahead of him, with whatever he wants to find here. For he jumped his bonus offer, right away, to twenty-five thousand dollars. If I'm any judge of such a man, I haven't heard the last of friend Laigne. He's out to make trouble. And he has some tremendous interest at stake."

"There's something else," said Wanda, hesitantly, "though I don't suppose it's at all significant. Only, I've wondered about it. You were speaking about John King a minute ago. When Mrs. Rance was so ill, down below here, she sent several times for Dad, late at night or early in the morning, thinking she was dying. I paddled Dad there and came back alone. Twice, early in the morning—before sunrise —when I was paddling past here on the way home from the Rance cabin, I saw John King come out of Sea-Dream House."

"But ——"

"Twice. Both times he let himself out as stealthily as a burglar, and he melted out of sight in the undergrowth. It seemed so queer to me! Probably he was just satisfying his curiosity by wandering through the house where old Laxahatchee is supposed to have been buried. But why should he do it at such an unearthly hour? There was nothing to pre-

vent his going there openly, by daylight
or ——"

"King?" repeated Tevvis, in wonder.
"You're certain? You're sure it wasn't some
one else?"

"Why, I've known John King ever since I
was a baby! Besides, is there anyone else who
looks a bit like him? Both times I saw his
face clearly. He ——"

"Miss Reeve," said Tevvis, "yesterday King
asked my leave to call on me some time and
explore Sea-Dream House. He said he broke
in there once when he was a child and got
whipped by his father for trespassing. He says
he was made to swear he'd never trespass there
again. That's why he wanted leave to come
to the house openly and explore it. Why
should he have told such a useless and silly
lie, if you really saw him come out of the
house, twice, lately?"

"He told you that?" she exclaimed, incredulous. "Why—you must have been mistaken!
He ——"

"He told me that," insisted Saul. "And

it adds another quaint angle to the situation. That makes at least four sets of people who seem anxious to wander undisturbed around this musty old ruin. King—Laigne—the treasure-hunting idiots—the bootleg crowd. Perhaps others. The bootleggers have the only logical reason for infesting the place. I gather King is well off, so he can't be mixed up with the bootleggers. And he is a man of education, so he can't be a treasure-hunter. He doesn't need such treasure, even if he didn't know it is nonsense to look for it. What is *he* looking for? All four factions seem to be seeking different things. This is beginning to get on my nerves."

"The river water is going to give you a nice attack of malaria unless you go in and get dry clothes and a rub-down," said Wanda. "And I must go now, too. . . . Will you lunch with Dad and me, this noon, Mr. Tevvis? *Please* say you will, and then I'll know I'm forgiven for making such an imbecile of myself yesterday."

"You couldn't keep me away. In fact, you

just barely saved me from the rudeness of inviting myself. I warn you, you are inviting a mosquito into your house by letting me come there. I am going to be a pest and come to see you just as often as you'll let me. And we can play detective, too, in trying to solve this crazy puzzle about Sea-Dream House."

"In the meantime," she said, with a touch of almost maternal concern in her voice—"in the meantime you're not to worry about all this melodrama crew of crackers. I'll have Dad read the riot act to them and I know they'll let you alone. But, oh, *don't* go on any more jungle walks till I have had a chance to speak to him. It makes me sick all over to think how near that bullet came to——"

"Please don't think of it any more then," he begged her. "My best Panama hat was mortally wounded, but that was the only casualty. And——there aren't any words to thank you for getting me out of that quicksand. I think you know how grateful I am, though. Because—all at once, life seems gorgeously worth living."

She flushed, then laughed embarrassedly, and swung the prow of her canoe upstream. Saul watched her slender figure out of sight, his heart in his eyes, an unbidden warmth counteracting the chill of his dousing. Then slowly he went back to the house and to a rub-down and dry clothes.

When he paddled back from his dizzily happy two hours at Boulding that afternoon, after his luncheon with Wanda and her father, he repaired to his study for one more effort at writing, though for some unaccountable reason he was far more in the mood for dreaming. But a new obstacle delayed his ascent.

A spruce and smug young man was waiting for him in the ivory-paneled reception room —a man whose hired launch rode at the pier and who introduced himself as Willis Venner, junior partner of the Palm Beach real-estate company through which Herne had leased the house for Saul. The guest proffered the immaculate business card of his firm, by way of credentials.

"Mr. Keith," he began, fidgeting, "I am here

to present my company's apologies for a blunder they made and my personal regrets at the inconvenience we must cause you. We have been looking up the docket concerning Sea-Dream House, and we are chagrined to find there is a clause which proves we had no legal authority to lease the house to you without consulting the Madrid heirs. We have cabled to them for formal permit to do so. Today we received a peremptory cable in reply—a most unnecessarily abusive cable, Mr. Keith —positively forbidding us to rent the place to anybody, as one of the heirs is coming over here to occupy it for a few months."

"How interesting!" commented Saul.

"How distressing!" corrected Venner. "It means we must ask you to vacate at once, Mr. Keith, much as it humiliates us. As I said, the entire fault is ours. So we shall, of course, not only return your rent money to you, but we shall endeavor to make up for whatever inconvenience we are causing you by adding a cash bonus of one thousand dollars to our refund. Again I tender the apologies of our firm—our sincerest regrets. And if you can make it wholly convenient to vacate by tomorrow ——"

"I can't!" snapped Tevvis. "In other words, I won't! I rented this house in good faith; and I paid my full rental in advance and received your company's signed lease. Everything was in legal order. Here I stay."

"But, Mr. Keith!" fumed the dapper little realtor. "I've just explained ——"

"You've just explained the details of a very clumsy lie, Mr. Venner. Norman Laigne hasn't wasted much time. The busy little brain is never still, eh? Always there with a bright answer. He went straight from me to you people today, and he threw so much cash into you that you forgot any fragments of business ethics you may ever have known ——"

"Mr. Keith! Oh, Mr. Keith!" disclaimed the virtuously indignant Venner. "I— we ——"

"Laigne has bribed you to get me out," averred Saul in grinning good humor as the fight zest began to tingle through him. "Laigne

and Laigne's cash framed this crooked stunt
—unless perhaps you are hired by still a fifth
faction? Well, to quote an ancient ultimatum
—'Here I am and here I stay.' I have possession. I have the legal documents giving
me that possession. I can spend a few thousand dollars, if I have to, to maintain my legal
rights here as lessee. I think that's all, you
poor petty crook. Also a thunderstorm seems
to be coming up. So clear out."

"Mr. Keith!" sputtered the scarlet and ges-
ticulating Venner. "This abusive language is
unwarranted. It is actionable. I shall ——"

"It is anything you care to call it," cheerily
agreed Saul. "But you'd be wise to act on
my advice and clear out while you can still
go with some dignity and under your own
steam. In ten seconds I shall whistle for my
collie. Bunty will ask nothing better than to
chase you into the river, at my order, deleting
sections of your nice clothes and your tidy
anatomy at every jump. Clear out!"

Chapter Eleven

P LEASANTLY exhilarated by his brief encounter with the real-estate man, Tevvis
made his interrupted way upstairs to the study.
There he found the circular room in some con-
fusion. Laboriously Gedge had dragged several heavy articles of furniture into it and was
piling them on the mosaic disc. He looked up,
sweating, from his toil, as Tevvis came in.

"What's the idea of the Leaning Tower of
Pisa?" queried Saul, surveying with no approval the pyramid of chairs and stands and
similar articles from the various rooms.

"You said to cover that man trap with
things that would be heavy enough to keep
folks from lifting it from below," Gedge defended his labors. "So I ———"

"So you're beguiling the glad hours by
making a Tower of Babel that's so shaky it
will tumble over at the first husky shove from

underneath," supplemented Tevvis. "Here, take all the rickety stuff away, and then lend me a hand with that big green sea-chest in my room. It has about a ton of iron junk in it, and the chest itself is mostly of iron. If we can drag that over the disc, it'll take plenty of strength to heave it up again."

"Yessir. But ——"

"The thing is too heavy for us to drag in here as it is. Come and help me dump out enough of its junk to make it lighter. Then we'll put it over the disc and you can pile the rest of the stuff back into it afterward. Hurry up. It's getting dark. There's a whopping thunderstorm coming along in a few minutes. Let's get the work done before it's too dim."

Gedge cleared his heap of heterogeneous articles from above the disc, grumbling fluently at the extra labor. Tevvis went into the adjoining room and across to the huge green chest.

He lifted its lid and stared down at the welter of aged bolts and hinges and broken tools and the like which reached wellnigh to

its very top. Then with both hands he began
to cast out the heavy stuff upon a sea-rug he
spread on the floor. The junk was rusted and
dusty and unpleasant to handle. Some of it
was light, some was hard to lift. Saul's hands
waxed filthy as he worked. Gladly he gave
over the dirty task to Gedge as the latter came
in from demolishing his carefully-erected furniture tower from above the disk.

Like the contents of the chests downstairs,
the surface of this junk heap had been picked
over and disarranged by old-time vandals.
But they did not seem to have carried on their
looting with any great thoroughness, perhaps
because the stuff seemed so worthless.

"Hello!" remarked Gedge, after he had
cleared away a layer or two of the rubbish.
"Here's a nice iron box, all carved and frescoed-
like. It'd make a grand bread box for the
kitchen if it wasn't so battered and dinged
in and all that. We need a good tight bread
box bad, in the kitchen, right now, what with
all those pesky ants and things. I've a mind

to take this and wash it and clean it up and use it. See, sir."

He lifted from the chest a disreputable old metal receptacle, about fifteen inches long by twelve inches wide and ten inches deep. It was unlocked, but a rotted leather thong was tied clumsily around it.

Saul took the box from the sweating old man, and was about to toss it down on the heaped junk upon the rug, when its weight told him the thing was not empty. He shook it. Something soft and not over-heavy wabbled about inside it. He broke the decayed thong and, with some trouble pulled up the dust-and-rust-caked lid. It occurred to him that the hinges responded to his tug more easily than they might have been expected to after two or three hundred years of disuse.

Inside was a thick packet of yellowed and stained and curling parchment, fastened together with a frayed and blackened silver ribbon. The dust-coated and half-indecipherable top sheet bore a faint network of crisscrossed lines and dots and crosses.

Instantly Saul Tevvis was alert with interest in his find. Here unmistakably was an ancient manuscript. Saul had seen top pages of antique manuscripts bearing this type of chart. One he had seen in a Spanish museum, at Cadiz, during a cruise.

Thus did many olden writers (and thus did such more modern authors and playwrights as W. S. Gilbert and Sardou) sketch on a separate sheet of paper their story's scenes or action-advance or character-development, to be used as a guide in the writing of the actual book or play. It is an idea not wholly unlike the first rough blue print made for an architect's guidance.

Here was a find, indeed—something to pore over and decipher in the lonely evenings when the day's writing was done and when only Gedge and Bunty were there to enliven Saul's loneliness! Tevvis was genuinely delighted. Then he fell a-pondering.

Had old Señor Don Lopez de Savedra been an author as well as a freebooter and all-around blackguard? Or was this a part of the loot of

some literary man's house? There was a tale
that he had slain an artistic Englishman somewhere in the West Indies and had gutted the
victim's house, even to the bronze name tablet.
Mr. Reeve had told Saul much about it at
lunch, that day.

But this could hardly be a manuscript written by the Englishman. For it was in Spanish.
The handwriting was all but letterpress clear,
despite the faded ink and yellowed parchment.
And it was unmistakably Spanish.

There were wide margins to the left side of
each of the stained pages which Saul was
riffling; and each page's writing extended flush
to the right-hand edge of the sheet. At the top
of the first, above the intricate lines and crosses,
was a vertical curlicue, more than an inch high,
that looked like a waterspout and apparently
had been drawn in abstraction of mind or else
to test out a new quill pen.

Saul carried the manuscript over to the nearest window; for the approach of the subtropic
thunderstorm was darkening the room to almost
complete twilight. Tevvis was not a brilliant

Spanish scholar. But he had a fair collegiate knowledge of the language; apart from such of it as he had picked up on his travels and the practice gained by more than a mere smattering of Spanish reading.

By the better light of the window he began to examine the topmost sheet, the page with the curlicue at the top and with the maze of guiding lines and crosses and dots below. It would be interesting to decipher this chart of scenes and action, sometime. He brushed away a wide smear of dust from the lower lefthand corner of the page.

Beneath, faint but legible, were tinily-penned words; some of them heavily, impatiently, crossed out and others substituted. Thus does a writer scribble and correct his first draft. Tevvis felt a kindred sentiment for the long-dead author. He sought to decipher the crossed-out and substituted words. Then he found they were proper names and were arranged in somewhat the order of a play's cast. With difficulty, and straining his eyes in the increasing gloom, he read:

"*Doña Clara—Doña Elvira*"—then both names were crossed off and in their place was substituted in triumphant distinctness, "*Doña Dulcinea del Toboso!*"

This final name had somehow a familiar lilt to Tevvis. But without stopping to cudgel his brains, he continued to read the next name or two.

"*Pedro Schanza*," he deciphered, though it was crossed off and directly after it was substituted, "*Sancho Panza, el rey del Barataria.*"

"By all that's incredible!" shouted Tevvis, in sudden exultation. "It's the original manuscript of Cervantes' *Don Quixote!* Lord! what a find!"

Gedge did not look up from his task of exhuming junk from the chest, but worked on as might a terrier that is called away from his efforts to dig out a woodchuck hole.

"What's that, sir?" he asked.

Tevvis did not reply. He was riffling the pages afresh—this manuscript of a book he had loved when he was a child. He was picking out once-familiar phrases here and there, and thrilling mildly whenever he came across a mention of the Knight of the Sorrowful Countenance, himself.

Evidently the immortal Cervantes had been none too neat in penning his book. Again and again words or whole sentences were crossed off and rewritten. The pages in some places were a veritable hodge-podge, while again, for nearly a whole chapter they were letterpress clear.

Saul rejoiced at this discovery. It would be a veritable literary education to him, in the stupid evenings, to study this manuscript and to try to ascertain why the Spanish genius had substituted certain phrases for others which he had written and then had rejected.

But that was all the discovery meant to Tevvis. Like most outdoor men, he knew little and cared less about the hobby of collecting rare books and manuscripts. Carelessly, now and then, he read in the newspapers of some sale wherein a Dickens serial first edition or a first imprint of *The Compleat Angler* was bought for a big sum. But it meant nothing to him.

The collector virus had not found its way into his veins.

If he had given the matter any thought at all, he might have hazarded the guess that this original manuscript of so famous a book as *Don Quixote* would be worth perhaps a hundred dollars or so to some museum or bookworm. It seemed an interesting curio; something to while away his own tiresome evenings at Sea-Dream House. That was all.

"While I'm willing to work my fingers to the bone, and while I've proved it many's the time since I took service with your late father and then with you, sir," whined Gedge, fretfully, "yet my rheumatics ain't any the better for all this lifting out of rubbidge from this measly chest. Maybe you'd care to bear a hand at it while I straighten the cricks out of my poor back, sir?"

Tevvis put the manuscript carefully back into its metal box and laid the box on the floor. Then, while Gedge stood up, straightening himself slowly and with lamentable groans, Saul continued the job of unloading enough of the green chest's load to make it easier to lug into the study.

Presently a tug at the lightened chest proved it was movable without too much strain for the mover. Alone, Tevvis dragged it after him through the doorway and into the circular room and directly over the center of the mosaic disc. Thence, in a succession of journeys, he proceeded to transfer the rug-load of junk into the chest.

Gedge, as ever, was as greedy for work as for complaint. He joined in the transferral labors, trotting back and forth with basketfuls of the iron refuse and dumping it into the fast-filling chest.

When the task was nearly accomplished, Tevvis left Gedge to finish it, and went to wash his own soiled and rust-stained hands. His pongee coat was stained and rumpled and dusty, from contact with the junk. He changed into a disreputably comfortable and shabby old shooting-jacket.

Then it occurred to him to go back into his bedroom and get the manuscript box; to carry it downstairs into the main hall and to set it on the table beside the reading-lamp there; so that it might be ready for his perusal that evening.

The box had vanished!

"Gedge!" called Tevvis. "Did you happen to take that battered tin box that had all those sheets of yellow parchment in it?"

"I sure did, sir," came Gedge's voice from the study. "You told me to finish dumping all the stuff back into this chest. The box was part of the junk—though it'd make a grand bread box, like I was telling you. I'm hoping I done right, sir. And I'm hoping, a lot more, that you ain't going to make me rummage down through all this pesky junk—me with the misery in my back so bad I can't hardly move— to fetch it out again for you. If you'd said you wanted it ——"

"Oh, never mind! Let it go!" Tevvis cut him short. "I'll dig down and get it, myself, when I want it. My hands are clean now, and I don't want to have to wash them twice in three minutes. It's too much trouble to get all hot and dirty, over again, just for the fun of spelling out a multitude of Spanish words. I'll wait till some other time. By the way, if the misery in your back ever eases up enough to let you lift anything as heavy as a needle, I wish you'd try your valeting skill on this shooting jacket of mine. It's all wearing out in the lining and one of the elbows needs darning. It wouldn't be the worse for pressing, either. No, don't bother about it now. Wait till I'm wearing something else!"

With an earth-shaking roar and a blinding quiver of pink-white glare and a rush of hissing rain, the thunderstorm burst upon the house. In all its subtropic fury it swept the jungle and the river. Terrific reverberations and sharp paper-like cracklings of thunder were continuous, and continuous were the stabbing flashes of lightning.

The rain hurled itself down from the dense black skies in a silver cataract. The river was whipped white by wind and by the downpour. The waterside trees bent and tossed and swayed as in a crazy dance. The rooms of Sea-Dream

House were alternately blind-black and blind-white. The house's stout timbers jarred to the impact of the thunderclaps. Every window was running like a waterfall, with avalanched rain.

Then, abruptly, as ever in the subtropics, the thunderstorm was gone, rolling out to sea, there to scourge shipping and at last to spend its remaining force on the shores of Bimini or of Nassau. But the rain continued, a sluicing and tireless downpour from lead-hued clouds.

The study was dust-hung and choking of atmosphere, from the much-disturbed contents of the green chest. Leaving Gedge to tidy it, Saul made his way down to the house's lower regions. Here was one more lost chance to work. But Tevvis told himself that even if the rain did not make the house too gloomy for good writing-light and even if his study were not a dust-clouded mess, he could not have concentrated on any worthwhile progress at his new book.

His mind kept reverting to Wanda Reeve, to the myriad inflections of her voice and the lights and shadows of expression that flitted across her dainty face with its tiptilted nose and its childlikeness of contour. No longer was Tevvis irritated at himself for this errant trend of his mind and heart. Unconsciously he had given up the struggle to keep Wanda out of his thoughts. Their queer half-hour at the pier, then his two-hour blissful visit at her home, had done unexplained things to him; things he did not try to analyze, but which all at once had become vital.

He and she had arranged for a fishing trip for the morrow—an all-day excursion on the Laxahatchee, carrying lunch along. Yes, it would mean another whole day lost from his work, but what did that matter, now? There were better things than work. Things a million times better.

Then there was this quadruple mystery hanging over Sea-Dream House: Laigne, sicking the smug little realtor onto him and wildly offering a twenty-five-thousand-dollar bonus for six months' occupancy of the dreary old ruin; John King, pretending to have kept away from the house since childhood because of a vow to his father, and yet having visited it repeatedly in secret and by night; the treasure-hunters with their silly rumor of a chart and their fear lest Saul might find the hoard ahead of them; the bootleg ring whose *caché* he had spoiled by coming here!

It was all so fantastic, so unreal! Yet, either all four factions were ludicrously on the wrong trail or else there must be something hidden hereabouts which made men risk fortune and murder in order to get it. The more Tevvis pondered on this—pacing aimlessly from one dim downstairs room to another—the more it caught his interest and curiosity. No longer did he look on the fourfold mystery with cranky impatience, but with an almost infantile craving to solve it.

Into the antique reception room he strayed, with its mildewed and frayed upholstered gilt chairs and its rococo mantel and its series of painted ivory wall panels set between bleached gold tapestry.

Panel after panel stared down at him, yellowed and with dim tracery of the cupids and

wreaths which once had adorned the ivory sur-
faces.

With his knuckles Saul Tevvis rapped idly
at the wall, tapping each panel in succession
in search of the secret passage whereof it might
perhaps be the door. At last, moving from left
to right, he came to the panel supporting the
scrolled Louis XIV mirror which crowned the
mantel.

A hard rap at this brought forth a rever-
berant echo, as if he had thumped a drum-
head.

Eager with curiosity at the hollow sound,
Saul searched in vain for a possible spring or
slide which might reveal a hidden opening
behind the panel.

Then, in a sudden gust of impatience, he
drove his muscular fist into the very center of
the mockingly secretive slab of ivory.

The damp-rotted panel did not split under
the crashing fist blow. Rather did its decayed
surface crumble and disintegrate. To the floor
showered a mass of smashed fragments of ivory,
revealing a deep hole behind them.

Out from this hollow leaped Something, not human, which launched itself downward at the dumfounded man, throwing fleshless arms about his neck, clattering all around him on the polished floor.

Saul cried out in sudden terror as the arms gripped his shrinking throat.

Chapter Twelve

A RIP of thunder sent the dim-lit house to shuddering to its very foundations. At the same time a lightning flare made the dark old room blindingly bright. They were afterguards of the spectacular electric storm which had passed on out to sea. In their wake the quietly sluicing rain continued to cascade down.

The interval of startling brightness had shown vividly to Saul Tevvis what manner of Thing it was which had burst through the smashed panel and had clattered against him in its floorward fall.

There, on the time-mellowed hardwood of the reception room floor, all about the astounded man, were strewn sections of what had been a human skeleton.

The fall and the sharp contact with the floor had smashed it into a score of fragments. The skull lay at Saul's feet, its sightless eye-sockets and fleshless jaws grinning up at him.

In the center of the skull's forehead was a faint imprint of a five-pointed star, stamped there by the instrument which had buckled and cracked the frontal bone and had caused as instant death, as does the pole-ax of a butcher.

Tevvis glanced, open-mouthed, from it up to the deep niche behind the panel. Another of Savedra's spooky hiding-places had been revealed to him. This panel doubtless had had somewhere a secret spring which caused it to slip back and to disclose the tall and narrow niche behind it.

Saul stooped and picked up the skull, carrying it to the window, whose musty velvet curtains he tore aside. That five-pointed star-mark was vaguely familiar to him. Then he remembered the meteorite ring with its raised star ornamentation—the ring Savedra had always worn on his right hand's middle finger and which no latter-day plunderer had ventured to steal from its brass dish.

"What a wallop the old murderer must have

packed!" mused Tevvis. "He struck just one blow—and it cracked his man's skull and killed him. He struck so hard that the star made a five-pointed dent in the living bone itself! Then Savedra got rid of his victim by sticking his body in that alcove up there and shutting the panel again. They couldn't hope to find him unless they tore down the whole house. Clever stunt!"

The rending of the dusty hangings let a wan gray light into the dim room. Saul laid down the skull and began to examine the other scattered bones. The body very evidently had been clad in a beaded robe and in other costly habiliments. For shreds of stuff and broken beads and the like were strewn on the floor, while more of them lay huddled in the bottom of the secret niche.

"Indian!" guessed Tevvis, examining bits of the rotten and bead-embroidered material. "An Indian of rank, at that, to judge from his clothes."

All at once the truth flashed on him, and he exclaimed, aloud:

"*Laxahatchee!*"

Reeve had told him of the sachem's last visit to Savedra and of how they were heard quarreling in this rococo reception room which was Savedra's pride; and of the servant's entering the room presently to find Laxahatchee gone. The mystery of the Seminole's disappearance was cleared up.

Carefully, almost reverently, Saul Tevvis began to gather together in a heap the strewn parts of the skeleton. He went to the niche itself and fingered the huddle of decaying clothes there for a possible missing fragment of bone. Groping amid the little pile of tinder-like cloth, his fingers closed on something oblong and flat and cold.

He drew it forth. From it dangled a wisp of rusted chain, almost as thin as silken thread.

This slablike object was no bone. Saul bore it to the window to study it more closely.

The thing was a pendant, apparently of unflawed aquamarine. It was perhaps two inches long by an inch and a half wide and a third of an inch thick. Its obverse side was deep-carved with undecipherable hieroglyphics. Its reverse was plain and was highly polished.

"This was an amulet," decided Tevvis. "The bit of chain proves it. It hung around Laxahatchee's neck, next to the skin. That's why the back of it is so polished. It's some kind of totem. Probably the thin chain broke when the skeleton came tumbling down, just now. It's—it's an exquisite piece of carving. Any museum would give a fortune for it. I wish I could decipher some of those signs on it. The Smithsonian could tell me what they mean."

Back to his memory came his talk with John King, and the last descendant of Laxahatchee's worshipful veneration of the old sachem. This amulet and the skeleton itself belonged to King, not to the finder. They must be returned to the heir, as soon as might be.

Saul wound the fragment of chain around the aquamarine slab and thrust the amulet into his coat's side pocket for safe-keeping. Then he went on with his task of collecting the bones and the shreds of garments into as decorous a heap as he could. Here he decided to leave his grisly find, and to paddle up to Boulding as soon as the weather should clear, to bear the tidings to John King. The trip would even give him an excuse to drop in on Wanda with his odd news.

As he turned to leave the gloomy room a long rapping sounded on the front-door knocker. Bracing himself for another nagging call from Venner or some new emissary of Norman Laigne's, Tevvis did not wait for Gedge to come down from cleaning the dust-clouded study or to emerge from the kitchen; but went, himself, to the door.

He flung open the portal, morbidly eager to give his frayed nerves an outlet by insulting the smug realtor. Instead, on the threshold stood John King.

The Indian was shrouded in a long black raincoat above his pongee suit—a coat which extended almost to the ground and from which rain water was trickling.

"Forgive me for bringing my wet self into your dry home, on such an afternoon," King greeted him. "I got caught by the storm down at Shuflin's, and on the way back I remembered your kind invitation to drop in on you and look over Sea-Dream House."

"For the first time since you were a little boy, I think you told me," answered Tevvis, recalling what Wanda had said of seeing the Seminole emerge stealthily from the house in earliest morning.

"For the first time since I was thrashed by my father," assented King. "I must have been under ten years old then."

"It's queer you've never been in here since," commented Saul, leading the way indoors, "when the house lay vacant so long."

"I think I told you," King reminded him, "I promised my father solemnly I never would trespass here again."

Tevvis was aware of a sudden contemptuous dislike for the gravely courteous liar. Masking his aversion, he helped King off with the voluminous and dripping black raincoat and spread the garment on a chair in the outer hallway.

King was looking about him with the frank interest of a child in a toy shop. Again that sting of contempt rankled in Saul's nerves, even while he gave due credit to the Seminole's powers of acting. Then he turned to his guest and said, hesitatingly:

"Before you begin your exploration of this house you haven't entered in thirty-odd years, I've something to say that may interest you. You'll remember you told me of Laxahatchee's last visit to Savedra and of his strange vanishing. Well, there's nothing strange about it any longer. It's all explained. He and Savedra had a quarrel and they came to blows. Savedra was wearing that huge knuckle-duster ring with the five-pointed star on it. He hit Laxahatchee in the forehead with it and fractured the skull. Then he hid the body in a secret niche behind one of the reception-room panels, and said the sachem had left the house."

In few words Saul told the tale of his experiences with the smashed panel. Again he gave homage to King's Indian self-control. By not one word or one change of expression did the Seminole give token of the stark excitement that must have been his.

"Come in there, if you like," finished Tevvis. "Everything is as it was, except that I have piled together the scattered bones and the rotted cloth, instead of leaving them strewn all over the room. It seemed more decorous. Come in."

He stood aside to let his guest precede him into the gray-lit room. With an inclination of the head, John King stalked past him and up to the heap on the floor. There King stood for an instant. Then he lifted the skull, picking it up with both hands as reverently as a priest might handle some holy relic.

As reverently he replaced it on the heap. Then, straightening, and throwing back his head, he stretched out both long arms over the bones and spoke three sentences in deep guttural. The words were in no language Tevvis had heard, and they were intoned with sonorous devoutness.

The courteous and highly-educated scientist had ceased, for the time, to be a representative of twentieth-century culture. At a breath he seemed to have cast away civilization's veneer and once more to be a Seminole medicine-man of five hundred years agone. Tevvis watched, fascinated.

As the echo of the solemn incantation died away, King faced his host.

"I ask leave to pray here alone, for a few minutes," he said, simply. "I wish to repeat above my ancestor's remains the sacred ritual of our people, which was denied to him in his hour of death. I am not only hereditary sachem, but hereditary high priest, of the Seminole nation. None but his descendant should speak above him the words which shall be his passport to our heaven. Will you leave me here?"

Embarrassed, half awed, much impressed, Saul Tevvis backed out of the room, softly shutting its door behind him. On tiptoe he made his way down the main hall, out of earshot. As he went, he could hear rhythmic and raucous chanting. But the sound came from the kitchen and not from the reception room.

Discordant notes floated out to the shocked Tevvis.

> "—— Came tripping daouwn.
> Away, away went Car-*o*-line
> Of Eedinborr ——"

"Gedge!" commanded Saul, bursting into the kitchen. "For the Lord's sake stop that caterwauling! How often do I have to tell you not to try to sing when I'm in earshot? Besides ——"

He broke off. Gedge looked around aggrievedly from a task which apparently he had been setting to music. Between the servant's knobbed knees was held a large metal box, very dirty and very rusty. With a cloth, Gedge was hard at work cleaning it.

"What have you got there?" demanded Saul.

"Don't you remember it?" queried Gedge, holding up the half-polished box proudly for inspection. "That's the one you asked me had I seen; and I told you I put it back in the chest with the other junk and I said it'd make a grand bread box to keep out these pesky ants and things. I got to thinking more and more what a fine bread box it'd be. So I digs it out again from under that junk, and I'm shining it up and cleaning it a bit with ——"

"Is the manuscript still in it?" asked Tevvis. "If it is, give it to me. I want to put it where I can go over it tonight. If you left the manuscript upstairs ——"

"Meaning all that mort of dirty yellow sheepskin paper, scribbled over in ink, in some furren language, sir? That wasn't no use to anyone. Just rubbidge. So I chucked it into the range here. My sakes! but it did smell something terrible while it was a-burning! I had to open the winders and —— I hope I ain't done wrong, sir?" he interrupted himself, at sight of Tevvis's glare.

"No, Gedge," groaned Saul, "you 'ain't done wrong'! In all the dreary years I've known you you never yet 'done wrong.' You're the one shiningly perfect soul on this wicked, wicked earth. All you've done, this time, is to destroy a valuable manuscript, written by one of the great men of all ages—a manuscript I was counting on getting a lot of pleasure and edu-

cation out of, during the next few evenings.
That's all. A manuscript that some collector
might have been glad to pay a hundred dollars
or more for. That ——''

"It was wrote in a furren language," Gedge
defended himself. "And it was all dirty and
faded. Nobody'd pay two cents for such trash.
You're a-having me on a bit, sir, I fancy. But
I'm sorry if I done wrong in ——''

The soft opening of the reception room door
caught Saul's notice. He hurried out into the
hall just in time to see King take the wet raincoat from its chair and carry it back into the
reception room, closing the door behind him.

For an instant Saul was puzzled. Then he
understood. The Seminole naturally would
want to bear his ancestor's bones away for
burial. This huge raincoat would make an
ideal receptacle, if it were gathered up at the
corners into an improvised bag. Unquestionably, that was why King had come forth to
get the coat.

Tevvis could hear his guest's light footfalls
moving from one part of the reception room

to another, as though the Indian were in eager search for something. Perhaps he was making certain that all the bones and other relics had been collected and no fragment overlooked.

The thought reminded Saul of the aquamarine amulet he himself had found and which he had dropped into the deep side pocket of the shabby old shooting coat he was wearing.

The engraved slab doubtless had been an important detail of Laxahatchee's dress or regalia. In any event, it was of value, both intrinsically and as an antique. Tevvis had read that such precious amulets used to be handed down from father to son among the ancient chiefs, for thousands of years, and that they were credited with almost supernatural qualities as fetiches or as talismans.

He put his hand far down into the deep pocket and felt for the amulet. He fished out a handkerchief, a pipe, a cigar-lighter, and two envelopes—the total contents of the baggy pocket.

But Laxahatchee's aquamarine amulet was not there!

Saul remembered with much distinctness that he had dropped the charm into this pocket, wrapping its broken thread of chain around the hieroglyphed slab. He had done it not ten minutes ago. It had not fallen to the floor. If it had, it would have clattered loudly against the bare boards.

It had gone into his pocket. No longer was it there.

He emptied the pocket and then turned it inside out. No, there was no hole in its bottom through which the lump of aquamarine could have worked its way. The inside-out pocket was empty. The lower seams were intact. The amulet was not in it.

Fancying he had dropped the thing into another pocket by mistake, Saul emptied and turned inside out every pocket in the whole coat. No result. No sign of the amulet.

It was gone—gone as completely as if the aquamarine and the gold of the chain had been made of ice. No, his pocket had not been picked. The only two people he had seen were

John King and Gedge. He had not been within three feet of either of them. Neither could have brushed against him and slid a skilled hand into his pocket, even if either had been able to guess he had had anything there worth stealing.

He had slipped the amulet—fully two inches long by an inch and a half wide by a third of an inch thick—into a holeless deep pocket, from which it had disappeared. That was the summing up of the happening.

Thus he could not return to John King the talisman which had been a part of King's ancestor's costume. Nor had he the nerve to go to that mourning high priest of the Seminole nation and say to him: "I found a large amulet among your ancestor's bones and clothing. I put it in my pocket. It has flown away."

Who would believe such an insane story? No, Saul must wait until he could find it again, if ever he could, and then he must give it to its rightful owner. In the meantime he could cause only disbelief and general unpleasantness by telling his incredible story.

As Tevvis stood there, uncomfortably, in the hall, the reception room door swung wide. Out across the threshold strode John King. Athwart his shoulder he carried his raincoat, bag fashion. It sagged from its pitiful burden of bones and rag fragments.

The Indian's face was pallid under its bronze. His eyes were hard and steely and they stared straight in front of him. His features were set and flinty. He moved with lithely noiseless action, as if through forest trails. By some miracle he seemed to be an aboriginal savage, out of place in his correct civilized garments.

As Tevvis came forward to meet his guest, a smolder flickered and burned in the Seminole's black eyes. There was murder lurking in their depths as they met Saul's.

"I am sorry I was so clumsy as to knock Laxahatchee's bones all over the place, that way," faltered Tevvis, seeking vainly a reason for King's new attitude toward him. "I gathered up everything, as best I could. I——"

John King stalked past him, without a word, passing out of the house and into the downpour of early dusk. A minute later, through the rain-haze, Tevvis could see him sitting straight and statuelike in the stern of his canoe, paddling it upstream with sweeping strokes.

And so the Seminole passed out of sight through the murk. Saul Tevvis returned, wondering, to the cheerless main hall. He was newly vexed with Gedge for burning up the Spanish manuscript whose perusal might well have whiled away a stupid hour or two for him before dinner time.

But much of his life was taken up with vexation at Gedge's thick-headedness and at the old fellow's genius for doing the wrong thing. Saul put the annoyance from his mind and sought to think of other matters. As usual, his thoughts swung back to Wanda.

As he stood there, frowning out at the rain, he heard distinctly the tread of light footsteps in the upper hallway. Thus did Gedge walk when he was remorseful at having done something to call forth a word of rebuke from his loved employer. His wonted shuffle ever turned to a hesitant tiptoeing at such times. Pitiably like the slinking of a scolded dog. Saul's conscience smote him for his own sarcastic ill-temper toward the old blunderer. From the foot of the stairs, he said, reassuringly:

"It's all right, Gedge. Don't worry about it any more. It doesn't matter. I——"

"Huh?" queried Gedge, sticking his head out through the half-open kitchen door. "Was you a-calling me, sir?"

For answer, Saul Tevvis sped up the stairway, three steps at a time. Arrived in the upper hall, he ran from room to room, through the gathering dusk. Nothing there, nobody there.

"Anything wrong, sir?" asked Gedge from the foot of the stairs.

"No," answered Tevvis. "Nothing wronger than usual. But there are more ends than one to a rat hole, it seems. And we stopped up only one of them today, when we put that weight on top of the mosaic disc."

From the gloom behind him something whizzed, like a giant hornet. At first breath of the sound Tevvis spun about. Something brushed past his face, imbedding itself in the newel-post of the stairhead, just behind him.

It was a thick knife, short and gleaming; and it quivered from the impact with the hard wood into which a half-inch of its point had stuck itself.

Tevvis rushed forward, toward the dark hallway corner whence the knife had been flung —the knife which had missed its mark by ever so little margin, because of his sudden shift of position.

There was a wainscoted space mortised together at the dim-seen corner—a space where stood a black Jacobean chair. As Tevvis charged at the dark corner, the chair spun forward, seemingly of its own volition, out of the dusk.

Skittering sideways, it smote the running

man just below both knees with a clattering force. Over he went, almost on his face, as its upthrust wooden legs tripped him.

With an impatient jerk Tevvis righted himself and kicked aside the big impeding chair. Then he dashed forward anew toward the black corner.

He reached it, and struck a light to see its details more clearly.

Nothing was there.

The Spanish-walnut wainscoting, darkened by centuries, ran halfway up the rough-cast wall, meeting in the corner with only a single seam. Nobody crouched there. No sound of feet could be heard in the further reaches of the hallway. Tevvis stood alone in the emptily sinister corner.

Gedge came floundering upstairs, a candle-stick in one uplifted hand, grease spattering him as he advanced. With him trotted Bunty. She had been out on a twilight prowl of the grounds and had just been let in at the kitchen door. The sound of the flung chair had aroused the worried curiosity of both dog and man and they were coming to investigate.

"What's gone wrong, sir?" asked the puffing Gedge.

"I've found another rat-hole entrance," returned Saul. "Bring that candle closer. See these panels where they join at the corner? One of them slides back, if we could work out the combination or find the spring. Where it leads to I don't know. But a kind neighbor happened to be traipsing around up here. When I caught him at it he threw a knife at me and then a chair. Then he ducked through the open panel and shut it behind him. By this time he's on the roof or in the cellar or out of the house. No use looking. But there *is* use in doing something else. Chase back to the kitchen and bring me a hammer and a dozen of the longest and strongest nails you can get hold of. Quick!"

"If it's the cur that slogged me from behind ——" said Gedge, belligerently, as he scowled at the blindly placid wainscot.

"Get the hammer and nails!" Saul bade him.

While Gedge was gone on his mission, Tevvis made use of the time to rap the wainscoting and to scan its every bevel, by the flickering candle light. But one rap sounded like another to him; nor could his experimental pushes and tugs move the heavy panels a fraction of an inch.

Chapter Thirteen

"I CAN'T get the secret of it," he told the excited Gedge, on the latter's return, "though Bunty keeps sniffing at the bottom of that left-hand panel. Give me the nails. Even if we can't find the hole we can stop it up."

Viciously he drove the long nails deep into each angle of the corner; then at the overlap of each of the converging panels of wainscot. He worked hard and efficiently, sending the steel points far into the tough and ancient walnut.

As he used his last nail of the handful Gedge had scooped from the tool chest, he stepped back, satisfied.

"The next person who tries to slide one of those panels back or forth," he announced, studying with grim pride his noisy handiwork, "is going to find his enterprise blocked by a bunch of four-inch nails that will hold it shut.

I don't know how it used to slide, or even which panel it is. But it isn't going to slide any more. One more rat hole blocked. At this rate, in a few days we'll have the whole lot closed. Now let's take a look at that knife sticking in the newel-post. If we were living in a nice dime novel, it would have the owner's initials and post-office address and passport photo on it, besides a mention of his favorite flower and some damning finger prints. Let's see."

But the knife told nothing, even on the closest inspection. It was wide and thick and short of blade, and sharpened to a razor edge and pin point. Such weapons may be bought by the gross at any sporting-goods store. It might well have belonged to a sailor or to a woodsman or to an amateur fisherman or to a camper. Apart from the unusual attention that had been paid to its sharpening, there was nothing to distinguish it from any other utility sheath-knife that costs two dollars at retail.

"I've read that the conchs are experts at knife-throwing," remarked Tevvis. "Probably Mr. Reeve hasn't had time to call them off yet. Or perhaps they've compromised by agreeing not to shoot me up any more and just use me for a knife target. Scared, Gedge?"

"No, sir, I ain't!" stoutly averred Gedge. "I'm only a bit low in my mind that I don't seem able to take a crack at that cuss who sneaked up on me and slogged me. Once I can do that, I'll be all right. Now, unless you're wanting more nails, I'll just be going back to getting dinner ready."

"But I do want more nails," said Saul. "A lot of the biggest you have. And a wide slab of wood, and that sheet of zinc you cover the kitchen table with. Better still, take the whole top off the table, zinc and all, and carry it into the reception room. That niche I broke into may connect with some wall passage, even if I spent a half-hour in trying to find a spring or hinge for it and couldn't. It isn't likely Savedra would have made just an alcove there, with no outlet from the back. I'm going to nail the table-top over it. Then, with the best knife in the world, nobody will be able to cut his way in or out."

Thus it was that the yellowed ivory panel and the later gaping hole in the reception-room wall were replaced, before dinner time, by an enormous and unsightly oblong of zinc and white wood, nailed clumsily but securely into position.

Saul took a morbid joy in these processes for rendering useless any secret passages he could locate. Presumably the folk who made nocturnal use of Sea-Dream House were familiar with these and made use of them to avoid discovery or to insure safe means of hiding. With one opening after another nailed tight, the indoor sport of exploring the mysterious house would grow less and less easy of achievement.

"I'm going to be away all day tomorrow on a picnic, Gedge," said Tevvis, as he sat down to dinner. "Fix up a lunch, early in the morning. Not thick sandwiches and chunks of meat and fat pickles and all that kind of abhorrent cave-man provender you prepare for me when I'm to eat in the open. Something more dainty and palatable, if you can bend your genius to such ladylike pursuits. Miss Reeve and I are going for a day's fishing."

"I didn't s'pose you was going fishing with a baboon, sir, nor yet with that he-Injun," sourly replied Gedge, nettled at the slur on his food-preparing ability. "Will it do if I trick up a snack like I used to fix for you and Miss Crale when you went on them hikes, back North?"

There was a glint of malice in the man's small eyes. Tevvis ignored the unpleasing reminder of his outings of earlier days. He was about to speak again when, far off, through the diminishing rain, came a dull rhythmic thudding.

Saul went to the open window, the better to listen. From the general direction of Boulding came the beat-beat-beat. Then it was picked up from westward, and then to the south and to the east; until the dripping darkness throbbed with the measured thudding.

From a vacation spent in the Black Hills as a boy, Saul read aright the iterant sound. In the Black Hills a war chief had died. His tribe were summoned by drum-beat to the funeral ceremonies. Through all the night the mourning drums had throbbed; even as now, through jungle and open, the Seminole mourning drums were wailing for Laxahatchee and were calling the long-dead sachem's scattered tribesmen to his burial.

Strewn through hundreds of miles of the Florida peninsula were the remnants of the once-mighty Seminole nation. Some dwelt in Indian villages, some on farms, some owned modern houses and motor-cars and bank accounts. Some were day laborers, some were semi-nomads. Civilization had shaped many of them to its mold.

But, tonight, at the throb of the flat drums, the Indians forgot they no longer were the tribal masters of wild Florida and that the white man swarmed over their lost domains. Singly, in groups, in ever-swelling bands, they flocked to the burial of their greatest sachem's bones, at the mandate of that sachem's last descendant, their hereditary overlord.

Throughout the long dark night beat the

horde of drums, for miles in every direction. Throughout the long dark night the tribe poured in to the trysting-place. Once more, for a span of hours, Florida was the land of the Seminole. Once more, for a span of hours, John King was the revered sachem and high priest of a primal tribe.

Day dawned fresh and glorious, after the rain; and Saul paddled eagerly up to Boulding for his fishing excursion with Wanda Reeve. Very dainty and sportsmanlike was she in her khaki dress with its high-laced little boots and its knot of scarlet ribbon at throat and belt. John King's house, as they passed it on the way to the river, was shuttered and lifeless.

"Nobody knows where the ceremony will be," Wanda said. "Perhaps back in some Everglade 'hummock' that has never yet been exploited by white men; perhaps in some other of the Seminoles' hallowed spots. But there is not an Indian to be found this morning anywhere. They have all gone to do honor to Laxahatchee and to Laxahatchee's last descendant."

"King has ——"

"By the way, last evening Dad sent for a dozen or more of the leading spirits among the crackers, and he talked to them like a Dutch uncle. He told them if a hair of your head is harmed by any of the lawless element here, Dad will leave Florida forever. He's not only their adored pastor, but he's the only physician they have any faith in. So that threat will be enough to keep you safe. By this time it is all over the Laxahatchee region. Even the bootleggers won't be able to bribe any cracker to injure you. As for the moonshiners—well, they're crackers, too, you know, and a single word from Dad would bring the revenue people down on them. They know it. It is the same with the treasure-hunting clique. They're to give up their search for the mythical hoard while you're here. Dad has given his word you are not after any of Savedra's buried fortune. And they believe him. Yes, the whole cracker clan will keep their hands off you from now on."

"Thanks," said Tevvis, then with seeming irrelevance: "See? I have a new fishing knife."

He drew from his belt the squat-bladed knife that had brushed his face in its whizzing flight through the air on the preceding afternoon.

"And thanks, all over again, for what your father has done for me," he continued. "It was mighty kind of him. Now let's forget that my loving neighbors ever decided to abate me, and let's have a gorgeous day. Want to bet on the first fish?"

When Saul Tevvis arrived at the Sea-Dream House pier, late in the afternoon, vacuously happy and full of aureate memories of his day with the girl of his heart, Gedge came down to the dock to meet him. Bunty frisked ahead of the servant, her bobbed tail awag and her deep eyes sparkling with joy at this reunion with the master who so cruelly had condemned her to the uninspiring company of Gedge all day.

"That noisy gentleman is at the house, sir," reported Gedge. "The big one. He's been here for two hours and more. He says he won't go away till he sees you. I just couldn't seem to get rid of him, nohow. Yonder's his launch, below there in the trees, with the boatman snoring his thick head off."

Annoyed that his rosy memories of Wanda must be smirched so soon by a colloquy with the importunate Norman Laigne, Saul handed Gedge his fishing-gear, then tramped across the lawn to the house. On the steps Laigne was awaiting him. The big man's florid face was haggard and sallow.

"I've called, first of all, to apologize for my violence when I was here before," began Laigne, as one who delivers a set speech, "and then to have a business talk with you, if I may."

There was something appealingly humble in his once-blustering manner, beyond the mere curb Laigne evidently was setting on his voice and demeanor. Saul eyed him with less active distaste than before. Nodding to a porch bench of ancient ship timber, set into the veranda wall, he motioned his guest to be seated. Pulling out a pipe and filling and lighting it, Tevvis sat down on the opposite bench.

"Fire away," he suggested, as Bunty curled herself at his feet and ignored with pointed aversion Laigne's invitingly snapping fingers. "Forget about the apology. This subtropic heat is apt to get on a stout man's temper and nerves, till he's acclimated to it. Now go ahead with the 'business talk.' But I can save your breath for you by telling you once more that I am staying on here for the winter."

"I ——"

"I am not getting out," pursued Tevvis. "Especially since you sicked that willie-boy of a Venner onto me. He tried to bluff me into thinking there was an error in granting me the lease. There was no error, and he knows it. Also I am going to fight it in every court, if he tries to go through with it. That will make the case drag on till long after my lease expires. Really, Mr. Laigne, that was a very stupid move of yours, if you'll let me say so. You might have known Venner couldn't bluff me into ——"

"A desperate man will do desperately foolish things," said Laigne, shamefacedly. "I was desperate. I am still desperate. But I've had time to think things over and to get back some of the common sense that put me where I am in the business world. So I've come to you to lay all my cards on the table."

"I think it's about time," acceded Saul, "though if you will pardon my saying so, I never yet knew any man to declare he was 'laying all his cards on the table,' who wasn't hiding at least one ace up his sleeve. Suppose you either shake out the ace or else lay down no cards at all?"

Laigne was not affronted by the suggestion. Indeed, any novice in physiognomy could have seen the big man was terribly in earnest and that he had no thought to spare for anything except his errand. Impressed by the visitor's humbly eager manner, Tevvis bade him get to the point.

"I'll make a long story as short as I can, Mr. Keith," began Laigne. "As you may have heard in New York, I am a collector of rare antiques. I collect, partly because it is my lifelong hobby and forte, and partly because a shrewd and expert collector can make a fortune by his fad. He can buy priceless things sometimes for a song, and sell them in the right quarter at an immense profit. I did that, for instance, when I picked up the Maximinian amphora in a backstreet antiquary shop in Rome. I had been on the track of it for a year. I paid eight hundred lire for it from the widow who had recently taken over the shop at her husband's death and who had no idea at all of the amphora's worth. I sold it to Hecksher Q. Gaddys, three months later, for sixty-nine thousand dollars. It is in a place of honor now in the Gaddys Memorial Museum, in New York. I mention this as one of many instances."

He paused and wiped the sweat from his face. Saul waited impatiently. He could not catch the drift of the preamble.

"An agent of mine in Spain," went on Laigne, "has been on the track of something for me for several years. Last week I had a report from him. You are conversant with the collector market for rare manuscripts, Mr. Keith?"

"I've read that first editions and original manuscripts sometimes bring good prices. I don't know much about such things, myself. To me, books are only valuable for what they may contain. The average original manuscript is a pest. Why do you ask?"

"My agent was on the track of the original manuscript of Cervantes' *Don Quixote*," explained Laigne, with elaborate show of unconcern and with his eyes so busy with the lighting of his cigar that he missed Tevvis's sudden stare of interest. "He heard a queer rigmarole about it, and afterward he was able to verify the fantastic yarn. He heard that Cervantes gave the manuscript to an English friend and patron who admired his work. This Englishman, Tallbot by name, took it to Jamaica, in the West Indies, where he kept it among other treasures. Along came Savedra, the pirate, and gutted and stripped the place in order to fill this Sea-Dream House of his with art treasures.   Savedra brought the manuscript here."

Saul nodded.   He began to understand a number of things which had puzzled him; notably how the manuscript of a literary genius happened to be tucked away in the junk chest of a pirate.

"Of course," said Laigne, "some of the stuff Savedra brought here has been stolen since then by local vandals.   But there is an overwhelming chance that none of them would have been interested in stealing a sheaf of parchment pages.   Also, the manuscript would not have seemed to a man of Savedra's character to be worth concealing.   So, the odds all are that the manuscript is still lying loose or in a case, somewhere among the masses of junk that this house is supposed to contain.   It is practically a certainty.   My agent even wrote me a description of the Cervantes dispatch box that Tallbot kept it in."

He paused, his pose of carelessness dropping away from him.   With sudden earnest appeal he bent toward Tevvis.

"Mr. Keith," he said, "I am a gambler by nature. I believed—I still believe—if I could rummage around this house for a few days, digging into the junk and going through every chest and cupboard—I believe I could lay my hands on that Cervantes manuscript."

"I doubt it," interposed Tevvis, cryptically.

"I am sure of it!" insisted Laigne. "My hunches never yet have failed me. And I have an overwhelming belief I could find that manuscript here. I *know* I could. That is not only a hunch, but good logic, too. That is why I hit on the plan of subletting the house from you. That is why—perhaps you noticed—I was so perturbed when you told me other people were searching here for something. I trust my Spanish agent. But he may have blabbed. If he has, any one of fifty other collectors or their agents would be hot on the trail at once.

"There is no time to waste. That is why I have come to you, this afternoon, without waiting for legal delays. I have come to make a clean breast of the case and to make a business proposition to you. If you will give me free access to this house for a day or two, so that I may conduct my search to its end—and if I find the manuscript, as I know I shall—I will pay you forty thousand dollars for the privilege. There! My cards are on the table, Mr. Keith."

Sweating, shaking, striving vainly for self-control, he bent forward to hear Saul's answer. Tevvis blinked dazedly at him. No, Laigne was neither drunk nor crazed. Despite his keen excitement, the man was very evidently sane and in deadly earnest.

The preposterous price he offered was in keeping with his earlier proffer of a cash bonus for the privilege of subletting Sea-Dream House. But—forty thousand dollars for a mere jumble of faded parchment pages! Tevvis tried to recall prices he had read as paid for ancient books and manuscripts. But he could remember no such sum as this.

"Do you actually mean to say you would be willing to pay forty thousand dollars for the original of *Don Quixote?*" he asked, unbelieving. "You certainly are willing to sacrifice much to gratify your fads, Mr. Laigne."

"Frankly," replied Laigne, "I can't afford any such price, just for the joy of adding such a treasure to my own collection. I wish, with all my heart, that I might. It would be a delight. No, this is one of my business ventures. If I can get hold of that Cervantes manuscript, and if it is in fairly legible condition—as of course it will be—I can sell it, through Rosenbach, at an advance of perhaps twenty-five per cent on my outlay. Perhaps even fifty per cent advance.

"In any case, it will be a very profitable venture to me, besides enhancing my prestige among all the collectors on earth. That means much to any collector, as you may realize. And the cash profit will be highly acceptable, too. I may even be able to hold out for seventy or seventy-five thousand dollars for it. Such prices have been paid before now. How about it? Is it a bargain, Mr. Keith?"

"No," answered Tevvis, slowly, "it isn't."

Laigne leaped to his feet, his face purpling, the veins standing out on his forehead.

"If you mean that you are planning to forestall me," he raged, "if you mean you are going to hunt for it yourself, I warn you ——"

"I am not interested in warnings, Mr. Laigne," Tevvis cut him short. "Perhaps because I have had over-many of them, of late. Besides, you can save yourself the trouble of mouthing this particular warning. Because I found the manuscript you're speaking of. And I found it just as you said it would be found —in a lot of junk. In a metal box with ——"

Laigne's knees gave way under him. He sat down suddenly and hard. The reaction turned his rubicund face to the color of raw veal. His jaw fell ajar. Then, in a trice, he was galvanized to excited new vigor.

"You've found it?" he croaked, standing tensely above Tevvis's bench. "You're not joking, man?"

"I'm not given to Grade-B jokes," said Saul; "but calm yourself a bit, please. I have a jolt for you. The ——"

"How much?" demanded Laigne, unheeding. "What will you sell it for? I'll give you my certified check for forty thousand dollars, as I agreed. I'll have the check here by twelve o'clock noon tomorrow. I——"

"No use," refused Tevvis. "I told you I have a jolt for——"

"Put a price on it, then," pleaded Laigne, pitifully eager. "Name your price. I'm no haggler. I'll pay up to fifty——"

"Pull yourself together!" commanded Tevvis, speaking as to a delirium patient. "Get this straight. I can't accept any price for it. Not only because it wouldn't be mine to sell, but because it isn't in existence any longer."

"You lie!" screamed Laigne. "It——"

"My friend," interrupted Tevvis, "when you're sane again I'll ask you to repeat that, so I can thrash you for saying it. I don't punch lunatics and drunks who insult me. I wait till they get their senses again. I've just told you the manuscript has been destroyed. You can believe that or not, as you like. But, to save further bellowings, I will prove it to you."

He drew forth an envelope and on its back he scrawled the words:

"Come out here and bring your new bread box with you."

Showing the babblingly incoherent Laigne what he had written, Saul chirped to Bunty. Putting the envelope between the collie's jaws, he said, distinctly:

"Gedge. Take it to *Gedge.*"

It was not the first or the two-hundredth time he had sent messages to his manservant by Bunty. Pleased, as always, to perform for the benefit of even a disliked stranger, the collie trotted proudly indoors, bearing the envelope in her mouth.

"You saw the note I sent my servant," said Tevvis. "When he comes out you can question him, yourself. You can bear witness there is no collusion between him and me and that we could not possibly have arranged beforehand what he is to say, because neither of us knew what you wanted here."

Laigne sat crouched clumsily forward, his thick lips ajar from his spasmodic breathing. His eyes were glazed. Tevvis watched him with reluctant pity. The solemn hush of a sun-bathed Florida late afternoon hung like a pall over the wilderness world, as the two men waited.

Muffled by closed doors, presently came a harsh shattering of the holy stillness. From the distant kitchen was wafted the raucous burden of a song. Gedge was setting his labors, once more, to music.

"—and faound Mayree dead, with the child still alive
Clawsped tight in the dead mawther's awms!
Haow must that stairn fawther have ——!"

The ditty ended in an audible grunt of annoyance. Bunty had delivered her message. Presently the shuffle of feet sounded near and nearer to the waiting men.

Out onto the porch came Gedge, enveloped in a large checked cooking apron and bearing with dignity the newly-polished metal box.

"You wanted me to fetch you this here, sir?" he asked, in sulky wonder.

"Yes," said Tevvis, "and I want you to answer this man's questions, if he cares to ask you any. He——"

Norman Laigne interrupted by lunging forward and seizing the box; at which he had been staring owlishly ever since Gedge came in sight. Heedless of the servant's snort of indignation, Laigne snatched the box from him, turning it over and over, noting its design and pattern and conformation as if checking up well-remembered items.

"Yes!" he blithered, pawing it. "That's the one! Everything just as my Spanish agent wrote about it! That's the box!"

As he spoke he was wrenching back the lid and staring into the shinily empty interior. Wheeling upon Gedge, he shouted:

"What was in this box when you found it? Speak up, my man!"

"Apart from me not being your man, sir," reproved Gedge, icily, "and apart from me not relishing being hollered at, I'll thank you not to go grabbing things out of my hands without so much as a civil 'by your leave.' Likewise, I ——"

The rebuking glare on his rough-hewn visage gave place to a smile of slavish adoration. Laigne had yanked forth a handful of bills and was thrusting them upon the surly oldster.

"Thanking you kindly, sir," smirked Gedge, folding and pocketing the gigantic tip with loving care, "and I see you're a real gentleman, after all. What was it you was pleased to be asking me, sir?"

"What was in this box?" demanded Laigne.

"Bread, sir. Today's baking, sir. Three loaves of it, sir. I took it out and wiped the box, when Mr. Tev—Mr. Garry Keith—sent Bunty for me, just now. Bread, sir. Fresh bread. That was all."

Laigne glared frantically at him, then forced himself to coolness.

"Where did you find this box?" he asked, as civilly as he could bring himself to speak through his tumult of soul.

"In a big green iron chest upstairs, sir," replied Gedge, fingering the bills in his pocket as though trying to count them by touch, "along with a mort of rubbidge and junk and such, sir. It——"

"Was it empty when you found it?" pursued Laigne, his voice muffled and thick.

"Yessir. That is to say, it didn't have nothing into it but a swad of waste paper—and a bunch of sheepskin sheets, all bound together like, with ribbon, sir; and a funny page on top with lines and maps and dots and so forth. The rest was just a passel of writing in a furren language. Hundreds of moldy pages of it. And——"

"What did you do with it?" panted Laigne. "Where is it now? What did——?"

"What *would* a body do with a mass of worthless trash like that, sir?" countered Gedge. "It would only have littered up my kitchen. I sticks it into the fire and gets rid of it, of course. The way that furren stuff smelt, sir, while it was a-burning, if you'll believe me, was——"

To Gedge's incredulous dismay, Norman

Laigne slumped to the bench as if his spinal column had been removed. The big man buried his fat face in his fat hands and broke into uncontrolled blubbering, the tears oozing from between his convulsively clasped fingers.

Chapter Fourteen

"HE DOESN'T need you any more, Gedge," said Tevvis, in a low tone. "Clear out."

To Saul, as to most normal humans, there was something hideous and mortifying in the sight of a grown man boo-hooing like a whipped baby. He did not wish another witness to share in the degrading spectacle.

Presently, as Laigne's violent weeping began to ebb to convulsive sobs, Tevvis spoke.

"For a man who talks so largely about paying forty thousand dollars for a single manuscript," said he, "you don't seem to be an especially good loser. Get hold of yourself and stop being a cry-baby. No disappointment is worth such sloppiness. Even forty thousand dollars ——"

Norman Laigne lifted a tear-streaked and

distorted face from his hands and stared wildly at Tevvis.

"Forty thousand dollars?" he repeated, his voice still unsteady and sob-tinged. "Forty thousand dollars, eh? Rosenbach himself said that if the complete *Don Quixote* manuscript could be found, in fair condition, it would sell for something close to FOUR MILLION dollars!"

"*What?*" gasped Tevvis.

"I said four million dollars!" reiterated Laigne, his voice scaling to something akin to a scream. "Four *million* dollars! And Rosenbach knows, better than any other expert this side of the Atlantic. You fool, did you think I was staking my time and my reputation for sanity on a measly few thousand dollars by yammering at you to let me get my hands on *Don Quixote?* This was the heaven-sent chance of a whole lifetime. It was more money than ever I'll see. It was all but in my own hands! And now—a cockney idiot and a kitchen fire and a bread box!!! I—he ——"

His ever more shrill tones strangled into a wordless cry. Stumbling, reeling, feebly he made his way across the lawn to his waiting launch. His wide shoulders were sagged and bent. His once springy step was a shamble. He seemed all at once very old and broken.

He did not look back, nor did Saul Tevvis seek to detain or to recall him. Saul stood staring after him dully, confused, his brain awhirl. He could not digest this preposterous thing he had just heard.

If it were true—and Laigne's worst enemy could not have doubted the collector's terrific earnestness and sincerity as he had mouthed the startling words—if that bunch of mildewed and yellowing parchment really had a market value of four million dollars ——

Tevvis shook himself impatiently, as one who seeks to banish an impossible dream. Yet something within him told him that Laigne had been speaking the truth. Small wonder the collector had gone to pieces at the knowledge that this inconceivable fortune had kindled a kitchen fire! Small wonder that earlier he had offered forty thousand dollars—a mere one per cent of the total value—to Saul for putting him in the way of obtaining it!

"Gedge," said Tevvis, strolling dazedly into the house and encountering the Englishman in the hall—"Gedge, once there was a woman named Cleopatra. She was a piker, Gedge. A village tightwad. The very best she could do was to melt a pearl that was worth only a petty four hundred and fifty thousand dollars, and then drink it. She was almost ninety per cent behind your record, Gedge. So cheer up."

"Begging your pardon, sir," remonstrated Gedge, "but you talk like you had caught some of that Laigne gentleman's queerness. As for Cleopatra, I don't relish none being compared to her, neither. Not that it's my place to criticize royalty, but I've read some about Cleopatra in a book. And the kindest thing I can say about her is that her home life wasn't to be compared to the late Queen Victorier's, sir. Would you be wanting some of them new-caught fish broiled for dinner, sir?"

"Yes," assented Saul, absently. "Broil them slowly,—over a four-million-dollar fire."

Followed three days of calm—days wherein Tevvis did not do a single page of work on his neglected novel, but during which his canoe's prow pointed at least twice a day toward Boulding, and wherein a new golden mist obscured the memory of the recent queer happenings at Sea-Dream House.

On the third night he went early to bed, and to sleep, that he might be fresh for another fishing trip with Wanda in the morning. Presently, he had a strange dream; akin to a nightmare. He dreamed that he was strapped into the wall-niche wherein the body of Laxahatchee had been immured for so long. Bunty, from somewhere near by, was growling at him. Try as he would, he could not free his hands and feet from the bonds.

A final wrenching effort made him sit bolt upright in bed. His hands and feet were not tied, but Bunty, at the bed-foot was growling with ever-increasing volume and menace. By the faint light from the window Saul could see the little collie standing rigid on the bed, ears pricked, hackles bristling.

No sound reached Tevvis's straining ears, save only the blended chirr of the night insects and the chuckling of the river against the pier. He was about to relax and to sink back to sleep when the house's silence was split by a yell.

It was a roughly indignant cry, mixed of surprise and anger, and most unmistakably it was from Gedge.

"The nightmare habit seems to have hit the old fool as hard as it hit me," thought Saul, grinning to himself in the dark.

The cry was not repeated. The ensuing stillness was tenfold heavier than before. To the listening Tevvis there was something sinister in it. Bunty had ceased to growl. At sound of Gedge's yell she had crouched as for a spring, facing the door and snarling softly to herself.

Saul got up, and started gropingly across the room. As at a signal, Bunty sprang from the foot of the bed and burst into a salvo of deafening barks. Saul's fingers closed around the door-knob of his clothes closet. To quiet the hysterically barking collie, he picked her up by the nape of the neck and deposited her in the closet, shutting the door behind her.

"Quiet in there!" he bade her. "You'll have Gedge awake and bouncing in to see if a bear is devouring me, if you keep up that racket. It's bad enough to have him screeching in a nightmare without having to explain to him there's nothing the matter. If you're going to bark like that every time he has a bad dream and calls out ———"

He finished the sentence with a cavernous yawn and turned back toward his bed, abandoning his idea of waking Gedge, as Bunty must already have done that. There was an almost inaudible sound behind him as of the knob of his bedroom door turning softly. So Gedge had been aroused, after all, and was coming in to find what had made Bunty bark! If so, good-by to any chance of Saul's getting to sleep again for another half-hour.

Tevvis was irritated at the old chap's elaborately cautious method of entering. To cut short the slow process, he went to the room door and flung it wide.

There was a blinding stab of flashlight in his very eyes. The doorway was thick-crowded with dark-faced men. As Tevvis winced under the sudden shock of light, a dozen hands gripped him. Before the astonished man could collect his senses he was borne backward, struggling, into the room. He crashed to the floor under the weight of silently attacking bodies.

There he writhed and fought in futile resistance, with men hanging to his arms and legs and kneeling on his heaving chest, cramping his athletic strength and pinioning him to helplessness.

No word was spoken by the skillful assailants. In grim silence they went at their work. Once Saul's left arm wrenched free, momentarily, from the multiple weight on it, and he drove his fist ferociously into the huddle of bodies above him. He felt it smite heavily against human flesh, and he heard a gasp of pain from some one in the group.

At the same time he wriggled one leg free and kicked out furiously. Again he felt the thumping contact with human flesh and again he heard a wordless gasp.

Then they were all over him, and deft fingers were passing and repassing a thin thong around his wrists, binding them tight together behind his back. He was trussed like a roasting fowl, powerless to tear free from the bonds that cut so cruelly and so deep into the flesh of his wrists; powerless to get his hands into action.

No attempt was made to fetter his feet, his conquerors evidently realizing that he could do no damage with these further than by a clumsy and easily avoidable kick. No word of command had been given. None had been needed. The whole plan of attack and of binding had been arranged, undoubtedly, beforehand, down to the least detail.

Panting, bruised, Saul strove afresh to rise from under his avalanche of foes. And now no resistance met his awkward attempt. The men had moved back from him. Their work was done. They could afford to let the prisoner stand up, helpless and bound. It mattered no longer whether he stood or lay. He was equally in their power, in either position.

From behind the shut closet door Bunty was scratching and whining and hurling herself madly against the unyielding panels.

"Quiet, there!" called Tevvis, imperatively.

He had no wish for her release. Should one of these men open the closet door, the game little collie would dash out to her master's aid. A single knife-thrust or a series of kicks would infallibly kill her. There was no sense in sacrificing his loved dog chum's life for nothing.

But there was one other bare chance for aid. In almost the same breath, and with a shout that jarred the whole room, Tevvis thundered:

"*Gedge!* Don't come here. Drop onto the shed roof from your window and get to Boulding. QUICK! Bring everyone you can find!"

It was impossible that Gedge should have slept through the rumpus. Probably the old man already was out of his own room and pattering along the hallway. The yelled command would be enough to set him into action and to send him scuttling for assistance.

Saul had feared lest a hand might be clapped silencingly over his mouth before the order could be shouted. But nobody there in the dark made any move to still his clamor. After that first brief glare of the flashlight, the room had been in dense blackness—a blackness in which the intruders had worked with entire ease.

Now, still moving with trained ease in the dark, one of them went over to the table and struck a match, lighting the strong reading-lamp. He removed from it the green shade. The room was flooded with a yellow radiance that brought into full view every detail of it and of its occupants.

Peering about him, Saul saw a group of nine or ten neatly dressed men clad in the Sunday attire of the Florida farmer. All were Seminole Indians.

One of them was stanching unobtrusively a badly broken nose. Another was nursing an injured arm. Tevvis's blow and kick had scored heavily.

Saul recognized none of the marauders. Having overcome and bound him, they seemed to bear him no further ill will, nor even to take the remotest personal interest in him. Clumped beside the tumbled bed they stood, glancing toward the door in stolid expectation. Tevvis's gaze followed theirs. Noiselessly, on the threshold, from the dark hallway, appeared John King. Two more Seminoles were just behind him. They were carrying something which gave forth smoke and odor.

King was dressed in close-fitting black. His feet were bare. He glanced at the Indians, then at the arm-trussed prisoner.

"King!" exclaimed Saul, in relief, hurrying toward him. "Thank the Lord, you got here in the very nick of time! I've been man-handled by these tribesmen of yours and they've tied me up. Will you order them away, please, and will you cut these mighty uncomfortable cords that are gouging my wrists? It was white of you to come here to my help. How did you find that they were going to ——?"

His impetuous forward progress had brought him close to King as he was speaking. The chief thrust the palm of one hand carelessly forward against Tevvis's chest. With a contemptuous shove he sent the pinioned Saul reeling far back into the room. By luck and balance-control, the astonished Tevvis barely avoided a sprawling fall on his back. He reddened with fury at the cowardly action and lurched forward again.

With a curt gesture King signaled to his men. Two of the group stepped swiftly up to Saul and, standing well aside to be out of reach of a possible kick, they grasped his shoulders, holding him moveless.

"And I thought you had heard about this outrage and that you had come to help me!" raged Tevvis, glaring at the imperturbable King. "You offered to do anything you could to be of use to me here, and I thought you were keeping your word. I didn't guess you were the filthy coward in command of this pleasant midnight outing."

King made no reply, but stood on the threshold, eyeing the purple and furious captive as he might have watched the antics of a tethered leopard.

"If you aren't yellow clean through," mouthed Saul, "and if you came here because you have some grudge against me, make your men cut me loose, and then stand up like a man, face to face and foot to foot, and fight me, you copper-faced Indian swine! Will you fight me? Will you and any two of your stinking mongrel ragamuffins stand up and fight me?"

Still, John King surveyed him, as in mildly pleased impersonal interest. Several of the Seminoles muttered and stirred at Saul's characterization of their worshiped chief and of themselves. A sharp glance from King turned them mute and moveless. The sachem's somber black eyes rested contemplatively, once more, upon the writhing and impotently raging Saul.

"I don't blame you for being afraid to fight me!" scoffed Tevvis, seeking wildly to scourge his captor into accepting his challenge and thus giving him a bare chance at battling his way out of the trap. "Never yet was there an Indian who wasn't too cowardly to stand up to a white man, unless the odds were at least twenty to one in his favor. That's the Indian of it! Cowards and mangy curs, all; from your nonsensical old nigger blackguard, Laxahatchee, down to your filthy self. When they educated *you* it was like educating a rattlesnake. A mucker of your kind has no place on earth; any more than your pariah dog ancestor, Laxahatchee, had. Let only one of my hands free and I'll ——"

This time the mutter and forward surge of two or three of the grouped Seminoles blurred Saul's taunting invective. The insult to their demigod, Laxahatchee, was wellnigh unendurable. Several of them spoke and understood English well enough to catch the purport of the black affront.

Again John King's commanding glance checked them. The chief's own eyes were smoldering and his teeth were set. The snarled abuse had pierced his stoicism. Yet his voice was heavy and unemotional as he broke silence for the first time.

"Mr. Garry Keith," said he, "you seem a very noisy and very ill-controlled young person. I honor you for your courage in defaming a man whose name you are not worthy to speak, and I understand your motive. But it will not avail you anything more than your collie's roarings in that closet yonder. I shall silence her, as presently I shall silence you."

For a minute Saul's sharp command had made the imprisoned Bunty cease her infuriated racket from behind the closet door. But at sound of Tevvis's voice raised in mad wrath against his captor, the little collie apparently thought fresh danger encompassed him, for she broke into spasms of growls and barks, and banged her light body afresh against the shut door in frantic efforts to come to his succor.

Now, turning to face the closet door, King made a queerly sibilant sound from between his set teeth. It was a marvelously perfect imitation of an enraged rattlesnake's hiss—deadly, menacing, sinister.

Instantly the uproar from the closet was hushed. Saul could hear Bunty shrinking back in sudden mortal fright against the clothes hanging there. A light flashed across his mind.

"It was *you!*" he exclaimed, with new understanding, as King turned back to him. "It was you who sent her flying out of the house in terror that evening when Gedge said he saw two luminous ghosts fighting, out in the hallway. It was you who rescued that conch boy I caught the other night. You knocked Gedge over the head and you made the hissing sound that paralyzed Bunty with fear. It was you, who ——"

"Most sensitive dogs, with strong ancestral instincts, are terrified at the hiss of a rattlesnake," assented King in prim diction. "But she is more so than any other dog I have seen. She has been bitten at some time by a rattler."

"And your radiolite experiments!" cried Tevvis, in another glint of inspiration. "You found a way to coat yourself with stuff, from radiolite, that made your body glow in the dark and scared silly people into thinking you were a ghost. That made your visits here safe. That and your knowledge of the secret panels and passages. Poor old Gedge! And I said he lied when he told me of two fiery ghosts fighting in the dark up here."

"It was not a fight," corrected John King. "A foolish treasure-hunting cracker met me in the hallway just as your man came up the stairs. We both made for the wainscot panel-opening at the same time. In the crowding together, some of the illumination was smeared from my clothes to his. Then came your dog, and I hissed at her. But we are wasting time."

Purposely Tevvis had sought to prolong the scene, that Gedge might have the more time to bring help. As though he read his prisoner's mind, King went on, in calm explanation:

"You wasted much breath when you bellowed for your servant to get out of the window and give the alarm. At that time he had been safely tied to his bed for several minutes. You may have heard his cry, or you may not, when he woke and before the gag could be slipped in place. Your Gedge is quite out of the situation. There is no one nearer than Boulding. One of my men is watching the river for chance passing boats. We are free from troublesome meddlers, Mr. Keith. Don't put yourself to the needless effort of hoping."

"But what is it all about?" queried Tevvis. "What have you against me? I have never wronged you. If you have any debt of hate to pay, are you too much of a poltroon to set me free and let me take my chance, here and now, with the whole wolf pack of you?"

"Why should I waste blood on what I can get for nothing?" countered the chief. "You say you have not wronged me. That is not true, and you know it is not true. Until you robbed me, I was inclined to be your friend. Indeed, if I had not disturbed the aim of Gramen, one of the best shots among the local bootleg ring's strong-arm men, you would have had a bullet through your head several days ago, Mr. Keith, instead of merely through your hat. I was returning home by a jungle trail

when I saw him ahead of me, covering some one
with his rifle. I saw it was you. I shot him
in the hand, just as he pulled trigger. It was
a trifling service—and I paid for it by a bad
bite in the leg from your hellcat of a collie,
before my hiss could send her galloping away
in fright. I tell you of the occurrence to prove
I was your well-wisher, until you defrauded me
of my birthright and repaid my friendliness by
sacrilegious theft. That is to be atoned for,
tonight."

"I ——"

"It may interest you to know the same
strong-arm man was paid by his employers to
come here and knife you. His throw missed
you—though he never misses. Thus far, you
seem to have been unduly fortunate, Mr.
Keith. But no run of good luck can last forever. The others were bunglers. I am not.
As you shall see."

He motioned the two men in the hall behind
him to come into the room.

"You are out of your head!" urged the
mystified Tevvis. "You say I have robbed you

and 'defrauded you of your birthright.' That is arrant idiocy. What are you talking about?"

"Presently," answered King, over his shoulder, as he stood aside for the two new-comers to enter.

Into the bedroom they came, bearing between them a table, whereon were ranged several instruments and bars and a coil of raw-hide. On the table's center was a deep brazier, red hot and heaped with coals.

Chapter Fifteen

A<small>T</small> K<small>ING</small>'s gesture, they placed their burden
in the middle of the room. At another
gesture from the chief, all but one of the dozen
Seminoles filed out silently. The remaining
tribesman shut the door behind them. Then
he stripped off the coat and shirt he wore and
stood naked to the waist, the upper half of
his body smeared with vari-colored paint in
curious designs.

"This man knows no English," said King,
pushing home the bolt of the door. "Most of
the others know more or less of it. I do not
wish them to hear. Besides, I shall need this
man. His trade is hereditary. He is the tribal
executioner—torturer, if you prefer. The two
come to the same, in the end."

Tevvis glanced toward the half-nude and
gayly painted savage. The fellow was busy
arranging articles on the table in whose center

glowed the brazier. Presently, he had finished his task, and he took up his station behind his chief.

"My people were adepts at torture, in the olden days, Mr. Keith," explained King, following Tevvis's horrified gaze with amused interest, "as you may have read. The ancient art has never been lost, but has been preserved from generation to generation. Sometimes there has been need for its practice, even as there is need tonight."

Saul Tevvis shut his eyes for a moment and prayed. Then he opened them again, his nerve rock-steady, his face unmoved. His glance was level and unafraid as he faced the stolid men in whose power he was. Never had he thought more swiftly and clearly. Never had he been less excited.

"Well?" he asked, his voice firm and even careless.

As he spoke he began to edge imperceptibly backward toward the torture table. Then, losing his balance, he lurched back and saved himself from a fall only by bracing his hips and his bound hands against the table corner. The jar of his impact shook the instruments on it and made the brazier tremble.

"Well?" he asked again, coolly, as he righted himself. "Does the murder begin at once, or are you going to satisfy my natural curiosity as to what 'sacrilegious' act of robbery I committed to merit all this elaborate stage-setting? I gather you are going to tell me, from your sending out of the room everyone who understands English. Fire away."

He shifted his position slightly, as if for greater ease, his bulk shielding from view the motions of his pinioned hands. His wrists were so close to the brazier that its heat stung them. By the greater or lesser intensity of the heat he was able to direct his motions.

Steeling himself to the almost unbearable pain, Tevvis maneuvered his tied wrists so that the narrow leeway of bonds between them should come directly above the glowing coals and so close as all but to touch them. His wrists were in excruciating agony from the fierce heat.

His hands had begun to grow numb from the tight-cutting cords. Now a flaming pain replaced the numbness. He tensed every nerve in his powerful body to stand the torture and to maintain a carelessly inquiring smile as he faced his captors.

"I am going to give you a chance, Mr. Keith," said King. "A thing my ancestors would not have done. If you will restore to me what you stole, you shall go free."

"That's several times you have talked cryptically about what I stole," rapped out Tevvis, his frown of vexation helped on vastly by the torment in his wrists and hands. "And I have told you I stole nothing of yours. Suppose we come down to cases?"

With a sigh of utter relief he felt the cords part from about his straining wrists. The fire had done its work, even as it had blistered the hands and wrists cruelly during the few seconds needed for scorching the connecting bonds in two. Keeping his released hands in the same position behind him, but farther away from the brazier, he repeated, in annoyance:

"What do you claim I have stolen that ——?"

"When you chanced upon the skeleton of my ancestor," said King, his black eyes seeking to read the white man's very soul, "you found something which no sachem of the Seminoles ever permitted to leave his body. That is why I know it was upon Laxahatchee, though my careful search could not disclose it. That is how I know you stole it."

"I stole nothing!" flared Tevvis. "I have no need to rifle a skeleton to get anything I need. What are you talking about?"

"From before the days when our history began," answered the other, "and before the days of the mound-builders, the king of my people was protected and was held firm in his sovereignty by the sacred amulet he wore about his neck and which never left his person until his eldest son and successor removed it after his death and wore it in turn. It had divinely mystic powers—sublime powers. You dull moderns who sneer at 'magic' cannot understand that or understand what its possession meant to our race. Laxahatchee was the last of our true kings. His body could not be found, for his son to take from it the amulet. Wherefore, from that day our race has declined, until now we are a scattered and dying people.

"If the amulet could be recovered and could be worn by the hereditary chief, its magic would still have power to lift us back to our olden greatness. I know it, even as my fathers knew it. To find that amulet, a thousandfold more than to find my ancestor's bones, I have searched this house of black misfortune a hundred times—the more eagerly when I found the house was to have a tenant who might blunder upon the talisman and defraud me of my life-hopes and defraud my people of their chance to rise from the mire into which your race has trampled them.

"You found that priceless amulet. I know you found it, for it could never have left Laxahatchee's living body. Nor would the drunken and blood-daft Savedra have known of its existence or troubled to search his dead victim for it. He would not have supposed a poor

Indian sachem could have anything secreted in his deerskin robes worth pillaging. Savedra's one thought was to escape the tribesmen's revenge by hiding the chief's body as quickly as he could. The amulet is gone. Nobody but you could have found and stolen it. That is why I am here, Mr. Keith."

The chief had spoken with a measured calmness, through which hot earnestness smoldered. Not once had his piercing black eyes left Tevvis's face.

Before the harangue was half finished, Saul understood its purport. A dozen times in the past few days he had racked his brain to account for the amazing disappearance of the slab of engraved aquamarine he had slipped into his shooting-coat pocket. High and low he had hunted for the lost amulet. Only fear of being laughed at for having to admit such an impossible occurrence as its vanishing had kept him from going to John King with the whole ridiculous yarn.

Yet now he knew full well that, should he tell this murderous Seminole the truth as to his finding and losing the talisman, he would be deemed a liar and the tortures would be applied in an attempt to make him confess where he had hidden it. Torture would be his until death should end his hideous sufferings.

Flexing his burnt hands he made answer:

"Yes, I found it. It was of aquamarine, with hieroglyphs on one side and worn smooth on the other. I put it in the pocket of a coat."

King's swarthy face was ghastly in its wild eagerness as he listened. The stoicism was wiped from it. Fearful must be the ensuing tortures the sachem would ordain for the supposed thief when he should hear the rest of the incredible tale.

"I put it in the pocket of an old coat," continued Tevvis. "Nobody would think of looking there for anything valuable. But if my life is at stake, I may as well come through with the truth. You'd find out, in two seconds, if I was lying. The coat is hanging in that closet behind you. It ——"

King wheeled about and reached the closet in a single stag-like bound, tearing open its door. The executioner, astounded by such un-dignified action on the part of his overlord, stared open-mouthed after him.

In the same instant, Saul Tevvis turned and snatched up with his blistered hands the heavy brazier. Disregarding the burns that seared his fingers almost to the bone, he swung the brazier aloft, and brought it down with all his mighty strength upon the torturer's bare head.

The man fell with a crash, the live coals cas-cading down over him and rolling in every direction. Some landed on the bed in falling. Others rolled under the window curtains.

But Saul did not wait to note the effect of his onslaught. Even as the brazier left his scorched hands, Tevvis rushed at John King.

King had torn wide the closet door, peering avidly in among the lines of hanging clothes. And out of her prison had slunk Bunty, still terrified and shaken by the recent sound of that dreaded hiss. But the sachem was as lightning-quick of thought and of action as the striking of the snake whose hiss he had emulated. More by instinct than from sound, he spun about in the closet doorway as the brazier smote his follower senseless.

As Tevvis sprang at him, King whipped out an automatic pistol from his pocket and leveled it.

Tevvis was upon him at the same time, and brought his right fist down with a smashing force on the chief's forearm. Before King could pull trigger the shock of the forearm blow had sent the weapon clattering to the floor.

In the same breath of time the two men clashed together in a death-grapple. Out from the closet they reeled, close-gripped, an avalanche of falling clothes following them. Across the room they battled, wrestling, striking, insane with blood lust.

Despite his slenderness, King was wirily strong and possessed of incredible quickness. Eel-like he twisted free from Tevvis's grip, seeking ever a hold that should master his stockier opponent. He was an inspired rough-and-tumble fighter, the most formidable antagonist Tevvis had met.

The coals had ignited the thin window curtains. Sheets of flame were soaring to the raftered ceiling. The bed and one of the chairs were ablaze. The room was thick with smoke reek.

Unheeding, the two foes battled on. King dived under Saul's left swing and sought the deadly underhold. Before he could gain it, a right upper cut had landed flush on his jaw, dropping him on all-fours. One of his hands clasped about the fallen pistol. Lightning-swift he lifted it and pulled trigger before so much as getting up from the floor. He aimed at the onrushing Tevvis, with barely five feet between them.

Bunty had been circling them as they fought, still cowed by the hiss, but eager to help her imperiled deity. Now, as King fell, she launched herself full at his throat. Her weight struck him across the arm and head, destroying his aim and sending the bullet wide.

Sharply he hissed. But now Bunty's knowledge of the death danger to Tevvis made her impervious to fright.

"Perfect love casteth out fear."

Furiously she drove at the rising Seminole's throat, afresh. As King thrust her aside, Saul Tevvis profited by the moment's respite to dive in and seize the pistol arm. Back he wrenched it, forcing the pistol once more from the chief's grasp. Foaming at the mouth, King leaped at him; caution and science flung to the winds. As he sprang, Tevvis set himself and struck.

King's jaw cracked under the fearful blow. His knees turned to tallow. He slumped face foremost to the floor, knocked clean out.

Through the eddying smoke of the blazing room Tevvis reeled to the closet and picked up from the threshold, at random, a pair of trousers and a coat. These he wriggled into, over his torn and bloody pajamas, thrusting his feet into house shoes. Then, pistol in hand and whistling Bunty to heel, he unbolted the door of the room. A mass of bodies were pressed close to the threshold as the Seminoles sought nervously to learn the meaning of the strange uproar from the apartment whence they had been exiled by their sachem's command.

Tevvis fired twice—thrice—into the thick of them; then plunged through their scattered formation, with Bunty close behind him.

To Gedge's room he ran at top speed. There lay the Englishman, tied and gagged and helpless. Saul swung him out of bed and to the window, letting the bound body down onto the sloping shed roof, whence it slid and bounced bruisingly to the shrubbery below. Bunty was flung out next. Then, his burned hands in agony, Saul followed.

Picking up the wiggling and wordlessly sputtering Gedge from among the bushes, Tevvis slung him over one shoulder and carried him, at a run, toward the pier. A dim human shape barred the way. Bunty snarled and sprang at the Seminole lookout. Saul fired in air. The shape vanished. In another minute Tevvis was in the motor-launch, with the bound manservant and Bunty, and was chugging upstream toward Boulding.

As they rounded the third twist of the river, Sea-Dream House came into view once more. From many windows, gushes of red flame illumined the night. The fire had reached the roof and had spread to other rooms than Tevvis's. Steadily the whole interior of the house was merging into a roaring furnace. The black sky was ever more and more deeply scarlet from the reflection of the holocaust.

Señor Don Lopez de Savedra's wilderness palace was perishing, like some hideously tormented living creature.

Chapter Sixteen

"AND I picked up one or two more bits of information from Gramen," observed the Reverend Mr. Reeve, coming into the parsonage living room, where Saul Tevvis lay stretched on a couch, his hands and wrists bandaged, while he dictated letters to Wanda. "When I threatened to have him jailed for his zealous efforts to shoot you and for throwing that knife at you, he turned meek. He told me several things he had picked up from his bootleg employers. One was that when the ring heard Sea-Dream House had been rented, they wired their New York man to find out who you were. He got into Musgrave Herne's office one night, and read Herne's private memoranda on the deal. That is how he found your real name and the name you adopted, and when you were to start South. It was he who put that note under the magazine in your drawing room.

Local members of the ring were responsible for the two other warnings.

"I know how the treasure chart rigmarole started, too. Gramen described the so-called 'chart,' from the description that's been handed down from the cracker who blundered across it. From what you told us about the Cervantes manuscript, he must have seen that first page, in the course of his rummaging—the page with the lines and dots and crosses on it. That's the traditional aspect of a pirate treasure chart, you know. . . . I thought you'd be interested. Don't let me keep you from your dictation."

He passed on. Saul started to feel in the pocket of his old shooting coat—the coat he had snatched up in his flight from Sea-Dream House—for his tobacco pouch. The motion of his hand made him wince. Instantly Wanda was all solicitude.

"How often will you keep forgetting that you mustn't try to reach into your pockets with your poor burned hand, you careless boy?" she demanded, with much severity. "I suppose it's

the pipe and tobacco pouch, as usual? Wait.
Let me get them out for you. Lie still."

She slipped her slender little hand into the
voluminous side pocket. Down sank the hand,
far and farther—more deep than even the
depth of the deepest shooting-coat pocket.
Then, puzzled, she withdrew her fingers. She
was clasping an oblong of aquamarine with a
tarnished wisp of gold chain wrapped around
it.

"The amulet!" babbled Tevvis, astounded.

Once more her hand was in his pocket.

"Look!" she commanded. "Up at the very
top, just under the flap, there's a slit that's
worn clear across. My hand went into it, instead of into the pocket itself. Just as the
amulet slipped into it when you dropped it in
there, that day. No wonder you couldn't find
it again! It was clear down by the hem, at the
very bottom of the coat, between the tweed and
the lining. Now what are we to do about it?"
she finished, turning the slab in her hands and
studying it curiously.

"Your father says John King has come back

from the hospital," said Tevvis, after a moment's worried thought. "Will you please have it sent over to him and let him know how it was found? It's his; not mine. Even if it can't do any of the magic things his ancestors thought it could, yet he's gone through a lot to get it. Let him have it. . . . That winds up the last detail of the wretched Sea-Dream House episode, thank Heaven!"

"Can you call it 'wound up' when your winter's work is all spoiled and when the doctor says you can't use your hand to write with for another whole month?" she asked, unhappily. "Oh, I wish you could dictate the book to me as you've dictated these business letters that had to be rushed off! By the way, have we finished them? If you'd like me to do any more, I'd be ever so glad to."

"Yes," said Tevvis, his eyes on hers. "There's one more. If you're sure you don't mind writing it. It's—it's the most important letter I ever had to send, in all my life, and I'm scared stiff over it."

"Can't it wait, then, till you're stronger?"

"No, it can't wait another day, another hour, another minute. Will you write it, Wanda?"

"Why, of course I will! Only, if it makes you so nervous and worried ——"

"It does. Ready to take dictation? Here goes: '*Sweetheart of mine* ——' Got that?

The girl paused, pen in air, her flower face suddenly blanched and sick. Then, by mighty effort, she wrote the dictated words, in a hand she strove pitifully to steady.

"Got that?" repeated Saul. "Go ahead, then, please: '*I love you. If you can't care for me, then I wish to God I had died in the Sea-Dream House fire, with your dear face before my heart's eyes. There's nothing but you in all the whole wide universe.*'

"That's all, I think," he said, as her heart-sick little face bent low over the page and as the faltering white fingers strove to trace the adoring words. "Please just sign my name to it, and address it to—'*Miss Wanda Reeve, Boulding, Florida.*'

"There! It's out at last! I —— Why,

girl of mine!" he broke off, in quick consternation. "You're crying!   I ——"

"Saul Tevvis!" she sobbed, in a burst of righteous indignation, as she hid in the bandaged arms that groped so awkwardly for her. "If ever again you frighten me so and make me so unhappy, I'll—I'll never speak to you as —as long as we're married!"